CHANDLE

Honey
Lump

A Historical, Biographical, Fiction

Outskirts Press, Inc.
Denver, Colorado

Honey Lump
A Historical, Biographical, Fiction
All Rights Reserved
Copyright © 2007 Chandler Fox
V2.0

Outskirts Press
http://www.outskirtspress.com

ISBN-10: 1-59800-743-2
ISBN-13: 978-1-59800-743-5

Outskirts Press and the "OP" logo are trademarks belonging to
Outskirts Press, Inc.

Printed in the United States of America

This book is dedicated to Lucille, Ollie, Verna and Dora; the four women who raised me to be strong.

I
LEGACY

It was 1913, October 26 Clarksdale, Mississippi. She was a blessed child born of a sacred forbidden love, but scorn as a bastard child of a bastard race, with skin pure as honey brown molasses rather than coffee extra creamed. She looked like her father's people though her complexion was tinted by hints of red hues; ancient Kemet was the dominant factor viewed as the X-factor and despised as a curse. Lucille was the legal name given her, but Honey Lump was her Indian name, which represented the quintessential essence of her persona, as well as the beauty she commanded. Now it was almost the turn of the century; and the way she entered this world seemed to be the way she would leave surrounded by turmoil and pain. Her strength now faint in the face of deaths angel she could hear the death bells toll as she stare out her bedroom window into the alley, with her expression blank she fearlessly measured, the merits of her life.

Lucille was created by a bloodline that carried traits of confusion denial and self- hatred mixed with a healthy dose of unadulterated pride. Her mother was of Indian and Jewish descent while her father was African. "The African" as family folklore described him seven feet tall and black as a star-less midnight. He tainted the family blood bringing abomination and disgrace upon the family's good name. The genetic pool had suffered irreparable damage now subject to the possible dominance of its recessive traits; which in America were as powerful as nuggets of gold buying greater acceptance and a lighter work load. All had been ruined and in the process they had lost their most beautiful daughter to the all encompassing powers of "The African".

She'd died trying to bare another one of his seeds an act that in its self is cursed by the heavens. She had broken Gods law of which she was not ignorant for Mr. Wright her Grandfather and owner of the plantation where she and her brothers were born and raised in North Carolina had taught them of Ham's curse. Their only defense now was to take Lucille and raise her up to fight against her inbred lazy, worthless tendencies. This meant never allowing "The African" to see her again. If at all possible they would have wiped clean any trace of this savage invasion but in order to maintain the honor of their lost woman child; Honey Lump would be allowed to wear "The African's" sir name, thus legally binding her to the proper name Lucille Ware.

She always felt conflicted by a great sense of family pride and her feelings of lowliness as a person. Lucille after all was literally the "black" sheep of her family. She looked different and behaved different. She was strong and defiant full of confidence and a sense of adventurous drive unheard of in the 1920's for a young black girl. Her earliest memory's as a child played on her inner self-esteem. In her grandmother's efforts to raise a proper young lady devoid of all Negroidness she inadvertently dealt blows to Honey Lump that would last a lifetime and ripple in waves through generations. Thinking back in time, she remembered the moment she first realized she was not the same as everyone else. She made the fatal mistake of licking her fingers, and Honey's grandmother said to her, "You want to eat like an animal you will not do so at my table. Get down on the floor and eat. Don't sit at my table until you stop acting like a starving nigger. I told your Mama about laying; down with dogs she didn't believe she would catch fleas. The more I try to teach you the more you stay the same, trifling; just like your old no good daddy and look just like him too, big and black."

Lucille was stunned and from that moment on she knew that she would have to make a place in the world for her self. Just seven years old and she already felt the weight of the world on her shoulders.

II
HONEY

In the early 1900's days passed slowly for a lowly black girl. But time had been Lucille's friend and in ten years she had blossomed into a beautiful young woman. Statuesque and voluptuous with a walk that startled men like thunder to a child. The sway of her hips combined with the power of legs that looked to be sculpted by Michael Angelo him self, rendered men helpless. Every movement appeared defined and intentional with an element of defiance and determination. She existed as an oxymoron black with soft hair, black and confident, black and unafraid, black, resilient, unashamed and beautiful. She was a rebel and a free spirit that was hindered only by a forceful undercurrent of anger.

In those days Honey hung with her cousin Doll who was pretty in that palatable way, fair with straight hair and a petite frame.

"Honey Lump!" called Doll as she entered the bedroom.

"Are you dressed yet? We don't want to be late for Mrs. Brown's lesson. I am not staying after today and cleaning that whole school house!"

"Doll please!" Honey exclaimed.

"I'm not paying that women no mind she know that I work the fields every morning before school and those books can't put no cash in my pocket."

Doll stood upright in her best uppity gal imitation and retorted, "Well she also know that a Wright woman does not have to work in the field and does so by choice."

Lucille combed her hair as she looked in the mirror ignoring Dolls presence and said, "That's right but I choose to smoke and go out on Friday nights too. That takes money. Besides I still get the best marks in school."

"Still I can't be late Honey, Doll pleaded."

"Mama is gonna let Erwin come by this evening for a visit and I have to finish that white dress I've been sewing so I can wear it tonight."

Lucille looked at Doll and rolled her eyes, "Girl I don't know what you see in him he so black you can get coal from him. I can't believe your Mama is going to let you take up company with a darky. I on the other hand will be out Saturday night with Tom Knollins, the most handsome man; in all the Delta. I don't waste my time with porch monkeys."

Doll conceded but continued to retort, "Now Honey I know Grand Mama is not going to let you go out on Saturday night. You are still in trouble for sneaking out last Sunday night."

"That's right Doll." Honey smugly answered, "and I will stay in trouble if that's what I have to do to see Tom."

"One day.... Doll warned, Honey you gone learn your lessons Tom Knollins ain't no good."

Lucille smiled slyly and quipped, "That's what you think Doll but he's good to me."

Both girls headed down the stairs in a fit of laughter as they made their way to school.

III

TOM

A tall slim cup of coffee extra cream with hair that waved like the ocean and a smile as white as piano keys accompanied by a voice that played a melody with every word he spoke. That's how Honey Lump viewed Tom Knollins the most handsome man in all the Delta and probably Jackson, Mississippi too. It was Saturday night and Lucille stared out the window as she washed the dishes day dreaming of Tom and thinking of the things they would do tonight. The late 1920's not only ushered in the Harlem Renaissance, but a rebirth throughout much of Black America, Clarksdale included. The music of rebel rousing youths at the time was a mixture of Gumbo with ingredients that melded the sounds of the slavery time field holler, blues, Caribbean Zydeco, Jazz and Gospel. She dreamed of the not so distant future when she would be in the throws of ecstasy dancing to rhythms unheard. At the local after hours juke, where everyone moved body parts they shouldn't winding round so close they touched, pelvic thrusts, wondering hands and enough moon shine to heighten or dull your senses depending on the ailment you needed to cure. Most people suffered from the white mans blues or heart ache while still a few needed to intensify the joy they had found in one another and this is where Lucille and Tom fit in.

Honey's grandmother was going through the final steps of her nightly ritual after a bath and hot tea she sat at her vanity and brushed her hair one hundred strokes. She had long black Indian hair that draped past her backside.

"Honey Lump" Her grandmother called! "You come make a palette on the floor here in my room, you ain't sneaking no where this evening ole fast tale girl."

"O.k. Mama," she replied.

The words brought a smile across Lucille's face. She knew that her grandmother was tired after a full day of washing and ironing. So much so that instead of walking the floors all night to make certain Honey was in her bedroom she believed she could steal a few moments of sleep and still listen out for any suspicious sounds or creaks in the floor of a sleeping house. Honey went to the linen closet and retrieved some bedding to make a palette. Her grandmother was already asleep. She loved her for she was the only mother she had ever known. Honey's mother had passed away when she was a year and nine months old. She kissed her grandmother's forehead dimmed the lamp and whispered, "Goodnight Mama."

Lucille could feel the butterflies fill her stomach as she made her way to Issaquena Street. The moon's light led the way illuminating the sky and Clarksdale Streets. She could see in the distance, fireworks of life bursting in the crisp Delta air. Fall was the season but summer's heat could be felt in the music of great blues singers Bessie Smith and, Howlin' Wolf who she knew as Chester. At the time he had a song out called "Moanin' at Midnight" and all she could think about was Tom when she heard it played. Honey smiled as she walked and hummed the moans in sync to the rhythm in her head. Lucille began to close in on Issaquena Street but Tom was no where to be seen. She became flooded with fear, anger and disappointment, her mind flashed back to the conversation she and Doll had Friday before school. Honey didn't want her cousin to be right about Tom being, "no good." Then from behind a tree she heard a familiar voice singing her favorite John Estes song, "Some of these women show do make me top dollar, a hand full of give me, a mouth full a much obliged; Well my Mama she don't allow me to fool round all night long."

She began to smile as Tom ran up behind her and took her in his arms spinning round and around.

"My sweet Honey" Tom said, "you made it."

"Don't call me that!" Lucille pouted while fighting a smile that curled in the corner of her lips revealing just how pleased she truly was to be with Tom.

He put Lucille down and stood as a proper gentlemen, Tom tipped his hat and asked, "My lady would you do me the honor of keeping my company this evening?"

"I don't know." Lucille replied slyly. "If I were to do you the honor, how might you entertain me?"

"Well now my good friend John here has a car and we are going with him and his girl over to Dockery Plantation to see Charley Patton, Henry Sloan and Howlin Wolf."

Lucille's eyes spread wide and tears began to well as she squealed with excitement smiling from ear to ear. If it were not for the Chap Stick she wore her lips would have split in the crisp cool autumn of Mississippi. Not only was she going to see the hottest blues men around but one of the brightest up and coming guitar players was driving her there. He carried himself like a man twenty years his senior, but John Lee Hooker was merely a boy, and man could he play that guitar.

Tom could see her joy and was pleased, "Honey would it be all right if I tasted the sweetness that one derives from a queen bee's nectar?" He toyed but at that moment Lucille would have given him anything, this man was flawless and smooth as butter with a tongue that produced the words of a poet. Honey melted in his arms and the passion of his kiss left her dizzy.

Tom knew exactly what he was doing and he knew that it would take a night of surreal mysticism, enthralled by the Delta Blues; conjured up in a juke joint of smoke and spirits, generated by moon shine to make a stallion like Lucille succumb to his will.

"Lucille," Tom beckoned. "Meet my good friend John Hooker he is going to let us ride with him and his girl over to Dockery Plantation."

Honey's eyes began to dance and her heart began to pound with excitement. She thought before that she might love Tom Knollins but now she was certain she did. John Hooker reached out his hand and Honey met him with hers.

He gently then proceeded to lift her hand to his lips. "Pleased, to meet you Lucille."

"Tom?" John asked.

"How you manage to pull a beauty like this man? She's a real dime peace."

"Now John don't you go gettin' no ideas about my lady, cause I might have to cut you."

"I know that's right." John laughingly agreed. "If I had a women like this I'd kill a brick about her."

Both men began to laugh as Lucille blushed. The young girl that accompanied John however was all frowns. He didn't even bother to introduce her to them.

Twenty minutes had passed but it felt like an eternity. It seemed that the car went looking for bumps and found every pothole from Clarksdale to Dockery Plantation. As they approached the town the sound of muffled music became clear and could be heard for miles around. Women were screaming and men were shouting; all in unison to the rhythm of the drum and pounding of the piano, it was Henry Sloan one of the best blues men of the entire Delta. They all exited the car hurriedly; fearful of missing even a moment of Henry's set. John stopped briefly to tell Tom that he would see him later. John had to meet up with the great Charlie Patton whom it was an honor for any young Delta blues player to do a set with. He tipped his hat to Honey and walked away with the stride of a rich man. The girl that was with him trailed behind like a lost puppy.

Tom grabbed Lucille's hand as they raced to the tenant's quarters. Dockery plantation was a huge farm that rented land to share croppers. On the weekends during harvest season; many blues musicians came from all around to entertain. These farmers had worked hard all year long and now they wanted to play hard. The money was good and the moonshine flowed all night long, while the blues played. Musicians were able to generate enough cash to have a decent meal and travel on to the next city or town maybe Memphis or Helena Arkansas. Many went on by train to cities like Chicago, New York, St. Louis or New Orleans. They were all looking to escape Jim Crow which was 20th century serfdom, with a mix of the slavery and cast systems all rolled up into one, under a different name but still the same.

Tom and Lucille danced until the end of Henry Sloan's set. Then Charlie Patton took the stage with John Hooker as his guitarist. The energy they created was pure fire. Bodies were swaying and hips were grinding; pressed together in a slow methodical motion that spoke what tongues dared to. During up-tempo tunes silhouettes moved in the same fashion but with a frenzied pace that dared a lover to revel in the moment's glory or be meted out unthinkable pleasures. After dancing half the night, Lucille and Tom slipped out from the tent for a breath of fresh air. Tom pulled a flask from the breast pocket of his jacket.

"You want a taste Honey?" He asked. Lucille had never drunk more than the sips all children sneak. She looked uncertain.

"Ah! Come on girl." Tom taunted. "I ain't gon let noth'n happen to you baby; I love you." Honey could hardly believe her ears it was like a dream. The whole night had been a never-ending fantasy. Before she could reply Tom kissed her softly on the lips and placed the flask in her hands. As she pulled away he nudged her hand and she began to drink. Lucille took four huge gulps and could not feel the stinging bite of the witch's brew until the last. Her senses had been dulled by Tom's words, which at that moment could have drowned out the sound of Gabriel's horn and she would have missed the Lord's Second Coming.

"Whoa, Honey you sure you never drank before?"

Tom joked as he took the flask away from Honey.

"That there is moon shine you gon' mess round and be cowboy drunk, girl."

The words broke Honey Lumps trance and she began to breathe again. Tom wrapped his arm around Lucille's shoulders and said, "Let's go back inside."

Once back inside the band was playing the kind of blues that makes a woman drink whiskey and a grown man cry. Howlin' Wolf, whom Lucille knew as Chester Brunett was just a few years older than she and had been well known in the black section of Clarksdale, he was a tall strapping man, somewhat handsome, with a smile that shined as bright as the beacons that guided the ships and barges through the mighty Delta waters at night. Chester had taken stage front and center sitting in with Charlie Patton's band. Honey Lump could see that John Hooker was now standing amongst the people surrounded by girls. There were so many that they pushed the one he brought with him to the back of the crowd reducing her status to that of a spectator. A silent calm, much like that which comes before the storm came over the multitude of lovers and happen stance couples as they pulled one another close.

Chester let out a moan, "Hemmmm, Hemmmm ……. Hemmmm, Hemmmm ……..."

Then the drum kicked in at a mid to slow tempo, and the guitar began to speak the lyric Chester hummed. He moaned with an intense urgency that lay some where between pleasure and pain. It was electrifying, generating a cross current of energy that made Lucille and Tom commit to a night sealed in ecstasy long before they made it to that empty tenants quarter they'd found. Tom looked into Honey's eyes and said, "I love you."

She returned his stare and replied with a gesture that said more than his words could ever communicate. Honey pulled one of the straps on her dress from her shoulder. She was a virgin making an action that stated simply; not only did she love Tom but she belonged to him and at that moment in that existence her commitment was forever. Honey was giving him a part of herself that, she could never, get back nor could she give again.

IV
AND BABY MAKES THREE

The sun was rising as Lucille crept in the back door still reeling from the night before; when suddenly she felt a stinging blow to the side of her face, it knocked her off her feet. Honey's moment of euphoria abruptly came to a halt. She looked up at the slight four-foot frame that housed her grandmother and wondered where all that power came from. The blow was followed by the words.

"You ain't nothing, but a street walker, a common whore lying out all night like an alley cat."

Then came the blunt trauma inflicted by a broom handle. Lucille didn't even raise her hand to block the blows nor did she speak a word or shed a tear. She was a woman now and would take her punishment as such.

Two months had passed and Honey had not seen Tom. She was on strict punishment and her, days were filled with chores, washing, cooking and cleaning. Her every move was monitored, Honey Lump's grandmother made her uncle, Walter "Bud" Wright, walk her to and from school. As they made their way down Paul Edward Street, Honey Lump's uncle and father figure Bud walked with pride and a great sense of importance. He carried a copy of the Crisis under his arm and always spoke of state of colored folks in America or other worldly events.

"You know Hun' Lump, we don't discipline you to be mean. I want the best for you and so does your Grandmother. Your mama was my baby sister and there was nothing in the world I wouldn't do for Ollie. She was the sweetest person and pretty as a porcelain doll. I wish you could have known her. You don't have many of her ways but you're headstrong just like she was. I feel like you are my baby. Sugar you don't know men they will take advantage of a beautiful young girl like you and make all sorts of promises they don't mean. I want better for you. There are young men and women who are getting their education and preparing to create a world for colored people where we can live like other folks and have the same rights. You can do almost anything a colored woman is capable of in this white mans world and everything a man can do on God's green earth; smart in your books too; but more than that you got good common sense and everybody ain't got that. The only thing that scare, me bout you is that a colored girl has got to have some sense of fear and you don't. You got too much warrior blood in ya. We Choctaw's don't always know when and where to pick our battles we so ready to fight we just do; and once we get started we don't know when to stop. Not to mention your daddy's side, he once told me that his father's father was feared and respected from villages all around in Africa, and that his tribe was one of the last strong holds to stand after the white man came. You know your daddy was born a slave and most of us didn't understand him. The women of the family thought he was mean because of his size and blackness. They thought he was ignorant too because he had been a slave, but your father is highly intelligent. He's just hard, but that ain't his fault, God did not make man to be broke like no horse. I know he love you and you should go see him."

Honey stared straight ahead with frowns of contempt and raging waters of fire welling in her eyes she responded coldly.

"I don't need to see him. I hate him. If it wasn't for him my mama would still be here. He's a stupid big black nigger, just like grand mama said."

"That's not true!" Bud interjected. "It's that kind of talk that lets me know you need to get out of here and go to college. You are half of what he is so what does that make you?"

Tears rolled down Honey's face as she turned in a tantrum to her uncle and cried out, "Nigger trash!"

"Don't say that word Honey Lump that's the white mans word. You are a beautiful young woman. You're prettier than any of these yellow gals and including the ones in this family. I know you ain't ashamed of who you are cause we raised you better than that. You are a Wright and even if you don't look just like us you walk like us and you talk like us ain't no quit in you and I love you for that. You got the strength of a man in your spirit and that's a hard pill for any real man to swallow. Most men's pride can't stand for a woman to out shine them. You have presence and that my dear can be a blessing viewed as a virtue or a curse that breads envy, jealousy and fear in men and women alike."

They both went silent and continued their walk in that state both knowing they had reached a stalemate and a truce forged on mutual respect. Bud was the only true man Honey had ever known. He was up right and true with knees that never bent and a head that could not be bowed. He was the provider of many, and a backbone of unyielding strength. And Bud knew that a woman like Honey was a rare find in the Delta or for that matter, all the world. She was not of mans rib but fashioned from a mold that God had broken a one of a kind who would always come to a fork in the road and keep straight with out giving it a second thought.

Later that evening Honey stood in the bathroom washing her face. She thought about the conversation she and Uncle Bud had on her walk home from school. She knew that she really was not angry with her Father but hurt. Honey had been hurt deeply by Tom. He was seeing another girl now and she was fair like him with long wavy hair. She felt in her heart that if only she had been blessed with a buttermilk complexion and her Grandmother's long jet-black

Indian hair Tom would still want to be with her. But it was the curse of her father that only allowed her good genes to permeate through the blackness as the red dirt of Alabama peers through the soil; but still it is, just what it is, dirt. Honey began to cry in silence as she felt the flutter of a jellyfish in her belly once more.

V
FISH FLUTTERS

Good morning, Grand Mama, how you feeling? Doll asked.

"I'm all right Doll, could be better if I could get that cousin of yours to mind."

"Honey gon' be all right Grand Mama, she makes the best marks in school and can whip almost any boy." Doll tried to put a bright spin on things. It only seemed to agitate her Grandmother more as she went into a tirade.

"That's the problem. You girls of today don't have a clue bout what it takes to get a man that's gon' take care of you. I reckon you may know more than Honey. I try telling that girl it's all right to be smart but even better to be a lady. Men want to feel needed. How is she gon' make a man feel needed if she can whip him? The man is supposed to protect the women. There are many things that I can do but I never let my husband in on it. Any idea I had that was better than his bout getting something done; I made him believe it was a notion of his. Honey don't understand she ain't gon' have it easy with men folks cause her mama took up with that African. If she don't look the part, she damn well better act the part. We Wrights' have a rich history and a name in Clarksdale she don't even understand her position; she been out there in that water melon patch. It's a disgrace. White man at the general store telling me how good a worker she is and how she can do the work of two men. I ain't raised no common field hands. We are an educated people. She gets all this from that African. Where is her pride? All I can do is pray. She can't help a lot of it cause it's in her blood."

"Now you, your way can be easy as you make it if you stop keeping company with the likes of that Dawkins boy, he and his whole family is black as tar. All you heifers is just determined to ruin this families bloodline. Things ain't what they was in my time. I married my cousin and have no shame in saying so. He carried the same blood as me. That black nigger blood is a destroyer. You all gone curse your kids. Get yourself a white man is what I say, and if you can't do that at least get somebody in your class. A white man will take care of you. A nigger man won't work and ain't gone do nothing but leave you with a house full of pick-a-nannies to feed."

Doll was simply stunned. All she did was say good morning and stop by to walk to school with Honey like she did every morning. She dared not to mouth off though. Grand Mama was good for slapping the taste out your mouth for smarting off and would cane you if she got mad enough. She was all of four feet tall but strong as a bull and swift as a cat. Finally there was a moment of silence muffled by an aura of disgust. Doll pounced on the moment, "Grand Mama you right and I do listen, but we gon' be late for school if we don't leave soon. She turned and went to the stairs calling up to Honey.

"Honey, Honey, Honey!" Doll called up the stairs. "You better come on we can not be late again this week. If we late again Mrs. Brown is going to make us stay after all next week and clean the schoolhouse. I don't want to clean that schoolhouse. I have things to do after school."

Honey yelled back in a tone filled with irritation and strain.

"I'm coming Doll but if you can't wait just go on with out me!"

Doll thought to herself that something did not sound right so she ran up stairs. She found Honey bent over the sink throwing up. "What's wrong Honey?" She gasped. "You sick?" Honey splashed some water on her face and rinsed her mouth out. She looked at Doll sideways with water dripping from her chin and said, "What does it look like?"

"Well did you tell Grand Mama Honey? You don't need to go to school sick like this. I'll go down and get Grand mama."

Honey grabbed Dolls arm and said, "Don't do that Doll."

"Why not, she'll know what to do for you, Honey."

Honey looked Doll dead in the eye and said, "There ain't nothing she can do for me."

"What are you talking about Honey?"

"I'm pregnant with Tom Knollin's baby."

"Oh no, Honey, have you told Tom?"

"Hell No! Doll and I won't. I don't need no man to help me take care of my baby and I ain't gone beg one to marry me. He ain't wanted me all this time no sense in him wanting me now." "But Honey he is the father, he got a right to know."

Honey strained in frustration as she leaned over the sink and hissed, "He ain't got no rights here Doll, and just because you make a baby it don't make a man no father. I should know look at mine." Honey Huffed. "Now, Doll you can't tell anybody I'm pregnant." She seemed to plead.

"I won't Honey." Doll replied with a fearful look in her eyes.

Honey stared at Doll and said.

"I don't believe you; swear it on the Bible."

Doll looked perturbed and shocked.

"Honey, that's blasphemy! But I promise I won't tell this one is going to the grave."

VI
BETRAYAL

Old Negro spirituals could be heard in the distance but Honey Lump was in another place. She could barely hear the painful undercurrent being song in unison that represented the pain of a people that still held hope for the future while knowing that the after life represented their just rewards. Honey was working at a feverish pace picking the cotton of two men. The more she picked the more she got paid and Honey was determined to make enough money to take care of her baby and rent a room. The dusk dark sky was quickly becoming morning's dawn and she needed to get home, the school day would begin soon. She wished she could work all day but that would lead every one to suspicion. Her plan was to not be living in her grandmother's house when every one found out she was carrying a bastard child. Just thinking about the disgrace she would bring brought tears to her eyes. Her grandmother had warned her even Doll had told her that Tom was no good; but she didn't listen. Why did she have to be so hard headed? She knew that she had been her own worst enemy.

"Honey, Honey! Come here gal!" The man on the horse called. "It's about time for you to head on to school."

He was one of those white men that stood one step up on the totem pole from niggers. His hair was unkempt and his English was broken, you could tell that he had no formal education; half the blacks on the plantation could read better than him thanks to the Freedman's Bureau. He was pure red neck and Lucille hated him.

"You bout the hardest working nigger gal I ever seen." He growled at Honey. "If things was the way they should be a white man could make his money a thousand times over off a heifer like you."

Lucille was not afraid to show her disdain and did so by staring the Ape-man dead on.

"Look at here bitch you still can get wiped. The only thing saving you is Mr. Johnson," he snarled.

Mr. Johnson owned the land she was working on and was quite friendly with her Uncle Bud. He told her uncle many times how good a worker she was and offered to hire her on as a cook once she finished her schooling. Her uncle always thanked him and replied, "My Honey's going to be a school teacher or a nurse; she's the brightest girl up at that there school."

Mr. Johnson would only laugh as if to say, keep on dreaming. He was a well intentioned, white man; but still a white man and he could not envision Negroes as anything but a slave or lowly laborer. It almost made Lucille sick to her stomach when thinking about it because now she knew Mr. Johnson would be right.

Honey walked the mile and a half hike back home. Two houses away she could hear arguing. It sounded like her Uncle Bud and Grandmother, but she knew her ears had to be playing tricks on her, because her uncle would never raise his voice to Mama. She rushed to the screen door and there she could see Tom. He was the tallest one in the house but the fear in his eyes made him look the smallest. Honey's Uncle Bud looked at her and said, "Lucille get in here! This young man says that you are carrying his child."

Honey was crying before he could complete the sentence. Her

grandmother screamed out, "Whore!"

Bud raised his voice, "Quiet Mama. Please!" Then he turned to Lucille with eyes sad as a gift less child on Christmas day.

"Honey, I told you that boys will take advantage of a girl like you if you are not careful."

He looked as if his dream had been stolen. He then turned his intentions to Tom.

"So young man what you plan on doing now that you got my niece into trouble?"

"I want to marry Honey." Tom said.

"No you don't." Honey retorted. "You want to marry your girlfriend."

"No, Honey I want to be with you. You having my baby and I'm a man; a man answers for his mistakes."

Honey was furious she looked Tom in his eyes and told him, "I don't want or need you Tom Knollins; you can hold your breath until you die waiting for the day I marry you."

Her Grandmother shouted, "You will marry him! I will die and go to hell before I let you disgrace this family."

Lucille screamed back, "I will not marry him!" and ran upstairs.

The others were left standing in the middle of the room in dead silence.

VII
VERNA

L ucille made it through the rest of her senior year and graduated. All the pomp and circumstance was bittersweet. Sweet because she attained what most people never thought she would. And not only the world but most of her family except, Uncle Bud. It was bitter because she and Doll were in the same class. Doll got the store bought dress for prom and all the accolades while Honey's indiscretions over shadowed her accomplishments. The baby was due any day now and her grandmother still wasn't speaking to her. She continued to refuse Tom's offer of marriage. She knew that he didn't love her and she now hated him. He was not a man of honor and she would not do him the honor of becoming his bride. She would rather wear the title of a loose woman than the Knollin's name. Honey's Uncle Bud had convinced her not to move into a boarding house after she informed him of her plan. He looked sad every time she saw him and she knew that he had forgiven her but he had not forgiven himself. He felt that he should have protected her better or been more watchful. He was the only father she had known and she knew he was hurting and that hurt her in turn.

Honey was lying in her bed staring at the ceiling as she heard, "Mama, Mama how you feeling?" The voice broke her dream.

"This is the last of your medicine Mama," her daughter informed.

"Verna is supposed to go to the drug store to pick up your prescription if we give her some gas money but this should hold you until she comes."

At this point the shots of morphine had become a formality that only dulled the pain but provided vivid pictures of the past that she could will to motion and relive. She felt a pinch and an oozing sting run through her veins as she floated to a time she and few others knew about. While she drifted back into past confusion she could hear the presents. In the other room some one was yelling.

"You ain't no damn good charging gas money......" the voice trailed off.

"Honey push!" the midwife commanded.

"I can't!" Honey screamed.

"You have to child you're a women, now!" Her grandmother yelled.

"Just give me one more big push, you can do it, the head is almost out."

The mid-wife's name was Odessa and Honey recognized her face from Mr. Johnson's plantation. She was almost blue she was so black but she had kind eyes and deep dimples with the whitest teeth you have ever seen. If she wasn't so big and black she could have been beautiful Honey thought. She gave one last push and called out to her maker.

"It's a girl!" Both women screamed.

The mid-wife washed the baby from head to toe; and seemed to fall in love; more deeply so with every stroke of the towel. The look in her eyes made Honey uncomfortable.

"Give me my baby." she seemed to plead rather than demand.

"This here is my baby." Her grandmother abruptly stated. "We will name her Verna; Verna Frank. I dreamed this baby was going to be a girl and they say you should flip your dream so I thought she would be a boy. I was going to name her Frank after your uncle we lost in the war. He was all man but he was beautiful and this child here is the same so she has to have some parts of his name. She looks just like her people."

Honey could see by looking into her grandmother's eyes that she was pleased and Honey felt a greater sense of acceptance. The curse of Honey's father had not passed on to her daughter. She was fair with straight hair and by looking at her ears she would not darken to a complexion past that of a golden brown in the summers rays. Honey had not yet held her baby, but that was all right because she felt reborn in her grandmother's joy.

Two days later Tom's mother came by.

"Hello, Honey, I'm Mrs. Knollins; Tom's mother. I hear I have a granddaughter here and I would like to see her."

She appeared to be a slight meek woman but strong and reserved in that society way. She never made indirect statements to get her point across but the meaning could be gathered in a pause or subtle nuance that made reference to appearances and the proper way. To sum it all up Mrs. Knollins wanted to see Honey and Tom married. He had been raised to take care of his responsibilities and to live a proper and decent life. This meant that he was not to father any children out of wed lock. Mrs. Knollins wanted to make it absolutely clear to Honey that Tom would marry her and never leave her side. Honey simply responded by lifting her nose as far as it could go in the air and stating, "I will not do Tom Knollins the honor of becoming his wife. The same dog won't bite me twice."

VIII
MA MA'S BABY

A year had passed and Verna was growing like a weed. She looked like a little porcelain doll. Honey allowed Tom's mother to spend time with her to much the chagrin of her grandmother. But she had been denied access to her father's people and she did not want the same for her child. They were after all decent people. This was as far as her parenting would go, because there wasn't much in the way of mothering Honey had to do. Her grandmother had taken the baby on as her own and often said, "This is Ma Ma's baby you can go on and do what you want. I'm gonna raise her the right way. She is going to be a proper young lady."

Honey didn't care that her grandmother had taken over the responsibility of raising Verna; in fact she felt it was for the best. She was not ready to be a mother and had never had any aspirations of becoming one. She decided that she would provide as much financial support as she could and would baby-sit when she had to. But she would allow her grandmother to be Mama.

Childbirth had been good for Honey's figure it brought on all of her womanly curves. She was now built just like a Coca-Cola bottle and this did not go unnoticed by the men of Clarksdale, Helena, or Memphis. Lucille had become a full blown woman and she felt in complete control of her life; not caring about others opinions or perceptions. She knew the power her physical presence held and used it to get what she wanted on her terms. She wielded her womanhood with authority and was merciless as she made mice of men. Tom had taught her a lesson in love but it was her Uncle Charlie that taught her the lessons of life.

Charlie was a smooth skinned, straight haired, impeccably dressed ladies man. He was well traveled in the military and spoke fluid French. He spent hours grooming himself and told Lucille that if you want someone to give you a million dollars you have to look like one. Women gave him love and money in exchange for empty promises and a dream. He had the uncanny ability to make believers and he knew that if someone believed in you enough they would do anything for you. He had seen it through out his life; soldiers believing in a commander and parishioners believing in a pastor all based on the promise of the fulfillment of a dream. Charlie was fearless in his escapades and didn't discriminate he dated old and young; black and white; mothers and daughters. If they could pay he was willing to play. He first learned of his ability to get what he wanted from women while stationed in France. The French women couldn't get enough of him. He was honeydew melon complexioned with a smile that was cunning yet charming. He didn't hate women but he simply viewed them as a means to an end. The only woman he loved was his mother. The only thing he loved was a well, tailored suit a fine hat and Italian shoes, but he was allergic to hard work. In the military blacks were treated like lackeys and janitors cleaning up after white regimens. After he left the military Charlie swore that he would not take anymore orders and would die on his own terms. Women were his hustle and he would rest and dress or lay and parlay. He saw Honey as others saw him, as a flawless beauty but a diamond in the rough. Lucille loved Charlie's flamboyant style. She admired his ability to articulate in such a manner that his words painted a picture. Charlie made you feel like you where a part of something big. The people of Clarksdale knew what kind of man he was, but they still respected him.

Honey was staring out the cafeteria window wondering what the future would hold and feeling hopelessly trapped when Charlie pulled up in his old Ford.

"Hun' Lump!" he called out. "Come on out here and talk to your uncle girl."

Honey went out the back door of the schoolhouse. There stood Charlie; as usual he looked like brand new money. He wore a brown pinstriped suit, with a brown and white polka dot tie accentuated by brown and white spectator shoes. He looked like a picture movie star and was dressed better than the wealthiest land barons in the Delta.

"Come give your uncle some sugar darlin", Charlie chimed.

Honey simply beamed with joy as all women did in Charlie's presence. He leaned forward and gently pecked Honey on the cheek.

"Honey I hear you working for that rich pecker-wood Mr. Johnson." Charlie began.

"Yes, Uncle," Lucille answered.

"Well I got a proposition for you." Charlie announced.

He went on to tell her how he had seen Mrs. Johnson at the market and how she couldn't keep her eyes off of him. He gave her his best step and fetch it act and all she could do was blush. He knew that she was ripe for the picking. Charlie's plan was to start picking Honey up every day from the Johnson's after she completed her morning kitchen duties at the plantation. He would then bring her back to the Johnson's to prepare dinner after she served lunch at the school cafeteria. He knew that if Mrs. Johnson became familiar with him he would become familiar with her. Honey agreed to the plot and; went on to inform him of Mrs. Johnson's drinking habit. For months Honey had been getting paid under the table to bring Mrs. Johnson her weekly supply of moonshine. The Johnson's had enough liquor stocked to get a hundred sailors drunk ten times over but she preferred old rock gut and didn't want her husband to know that his prim and proper high society wife was a lush.

"I knew there was something about the old gal!" Charlie exclaimed while nodding his head in acknowledgment and rubbing his hands together in a devilish wring. Honey could see the wheels turning in his mind.

It was exciting to be in cahoots with Charlie. "I'll be round about ten o'clock tomorrow; all right? Charlie confirmed.

"All right," Lucille replied with glee. "Is there anything you need me to do?" She asked.

"No little darlin," Charlie answered.

"All I need is a reason for being there and the rest will come. By the way Honey here's a five for your trouble".

"Oh, no Uncle you don't have to do that!" Honey rebuffed.

"Yes I do", Charlie interjected.

"Look here Honey, I'm gone teach you about the world and how it work. You are too pretty to struggle. We are too good lookin' to work hard. Any time a man asks you for conversation, don't leave empty handed. If he wants anything more than that make him pay his weight in gold up front. Now here take this five dollars and from now on don't let these niggers or rednecks talk to you without paying for it by money or trade. You hear me?"

"I hear you Uncle Charlie", Honey replied.

It was a lesson she never forgot; though it was a dangerous rule to live by.

IX
LET THE GAMES BEGIN!

Monday morning was a new beginning. Lucille felt reborn and in control of her own destiny. She hadn't felt that way since she first met Tom. She walked the half-mile hike over to the Johnson's in the haze of dawn; wearing the black maids uniform Mrs. Johnson had given her. There was a chill in the air but the smell of early morning dew seemed to offer a promise of renewal and adventure. Honey entered through the servant's way and began her day by heating the oven and lighting the stove. She would prepare bacon, ham, eggs, and grits. She placed the kettle on the stove to heat water for tea. Then she tied a white apron around her waist and began to mead the flower to make doe for biscuits.

Today she moved with a sense of purpose and authority. She knew that Charlie's plan promised death by lynching if they were caught but she also felt a sense of empowerment after feeling helpless for so long: living at the mercy of men and cow towing to white women. A second class citizen because she was colored and second best with in her own race because she bared the skin of her African father. It was ten o'clock and Charlie had been waiting outside the service entrance for almost an hour. He was leaning up against his old Ford smoking a cigarette. His car shined so that the glare from the window reflected by the sun was blinding. He was wearing a Navy blue double-breasted suit that hung perfectly from his slender frame. His clothes seemed to lay on him. He always accessorized with a matching hat, suspenders and shoes. But his ties and socks were in steep contrast; flashy or bright and bold. They added to his aura of worldliness. He personified the garden's forbidden fruit. Honey had noticed Mrs. Johnson's frequent trips to the window and knew that she was watching Charlie.

"I'm going over to the schoolhouse now Mrs. Johnson. Is there anything you need while I'm out?" Lucille asked.

Mrs. Johnson turned from the window startled and flustered; sweat was evident on her brow. "Why yes, Honey. Could you bring me some of my medicine? I'm almost out." Mrs. Johnson requested.

"Yes Ma'am, but I'll be a little late with dinner since we have to go over to the round yard to get it."

"That's quite all right Lucille," Mrs. Johnson answered. "But who is this we have here?" She asked while patting her long skinny neck with a handkerchief.

"My Uncle Charlie," Honey replied.

"Your Uncle Charlie?" Mrs. Johnson repeated as she inquired.

"Why, yes Ma'am, he is the one who gets it for me; he's waiting outside, now."

"Oh, well I hope you haven't revealed our little secret, Lucille."

"Oh! No! Ma'am, never!" Lucille shrilled in her best loyal Negress voice.

"I was wondering who that strange Negro was outside my window. I thought that perhaps he was your Bo. I'm glad to hear he's not. I wouldn't want you to get in trouble again." Mrs. Johnson sighed in relief as the redness in her cheeks began to fade away. Lucille could tell the sigh was not from relief of worry about her well being but a sigh hinged on hope, perhaps of things to come.

Honey was almost dizzy with excitement as she hurried to Charlie's car.

"Hey there sugar!" Charlie greeted; tipping his hat to Lucille and opening the passenger door for her. He was behaving like, the perfect gentlemen and treating her like a lady. Mrs. Johnson was watching from behind the curtains and fanning herself with a handkerchief. Honey and Charlie laughed all the way to the school as she told him how the lady of the house paced the floor frantically like a bitch in heat.

"She was so red, uncle when I walked in the room and asked her if she needed anything while I was out. She even tried to avoid asking me about you, but you know how white folk's is especially if they think there's some strange nigger hanging around their property. They don't go through no body else to ask you your business. She just knew she was wrong in her thinking and must have thought that I could read her mind. She like you uncle and even a blind man can see that, but how you gon' approach her?"

"I won't have to Honey," Charlie stated rather matter-of-factly.

"See what you have to realize is that she has all the power, but she feels powerless. The white man has placed her up on a throne but won't let her rule anything of any importance. Sure she can order a maid around or put a field hand in his place but that's petty. A lady like that has been barking orders since she was a child. She's ready to take control the only problem is she don't know what she wants to take control of, but I do. It's the same thing you and I want to have control over, and that is us. Her life is lonely and boring. All the excitement her man has to give; he given it to some whore or some field gal. He thinks that's how a gentleman treats a delicate white lady. He doesn't want to subject her to his perverse side but what he doesn't know is that she has the same needs and desires as him. It's just that people have been telling her to be a lady her whole life. I'm not gon' treat her like a lady. I'm gon' treat her like a woman. If you learn but one thing from today remember that men and women want the same things; now what it takes to fulfill those desires can be as different as night and day or one and the same, but that all boils down to the individual preference. If you treat a man like a man and be a woman that carries herself like a lady, but thinks like a man, you will have complete control. Just remember the things that mean the most to you mean the least to us."

Honey thought about what Charlie was saying and began to understand what her Grandmother and Uncle Bud had been trying to say. The mystery behind Tom's actions became as clear as day and Honey felt empowered. But she wondered why, hadn't any one explained it to her in this way before.

Three weeks had passed and as usual Lucille's ride had come to pick her up. Charlie was waiting outside the Johnson's by the servant's entrance. He had changed his attire for the evening and was now dressed in a single button gray suit with cobalt blue tie. The watch on his arm sparkled like crystal on a chandelier. He was clean shaven and his hair with its natural conk waved like the black waters of the night's ocean. His skin was flawless and the brightness of his teeth when he smiled lit up his face like the luminous glow of the moon. He was perfect. This had to have been what God meant when he said that he made man in his image.

Honey was cleaning the kitchen while Mrs. Johnson was partaking in an after dinner drink or two or three. Lucille made sure she bought the strongest moonshine Earl Lee, the round yard snake oil man had. Honey cracked the kitchen door and peered through to see Mrs. Johnson drinking what the locals called rock gut. She was drinking it straight with out so much as a wince or a frown. Her brow was wet from perspiration as she stared out the window at Charlie with reckless abandonment. Mr. Johnson had once again not shown up for dinner and instead sent one of the young field hands over to say that he would be working late. Mrs. Johnson knew he was lying and also knew just where to find him. He was at Adeline's house. She was a Louisiana Creole woman and many thought she had put a root on him. But Mrs. Johnson knew better. Her husband was in love and not with her. He hadn't sought her affections in almost a year. Half the time he didn't come home and when he was there he slept in his study; claiming to fall asleep while going over the books. She was lonely. Mrs. Johnson called out in the middle of her thoughts, "Honey!"

"Yes, Ma'am," Honey replied.

"If it's going to take you much longer, you can have your uncle wait in the parlor." Mrs. Johnson offered.

"Thank you Ma'am." Honey replied. "I still have to do the floor in here. Should I go get him?"

"It's completely up to you dear," Mrs. Johnson replied in an effort to remove herself from the situation.

"Well I don't want to impose. Besides he will be all right. I usually take him a drink of water about this time that should do."

"If I thought it was an imposition I wouldn't have made the offer. You should be just a little more grateful, with your uncle taking time out of his busy schedule to run you around. I'll go and tell him myself; because if you don't appreciate it, I do. At least you are not late anymore and I can have my meals on time. You know it's not good for the digestive system eating at all different times of the day." Lucille could hardly contain her laughter as Mrs. Johnson pushed past her and out the back door.

Charlie could hear footsteps coming up behind him, but didn't turn around assuming it was Honey. "You ready to go?" He asked after he took a last long drag on his cigarette before flicking the butt away.

Mrs. Johnson did not interject but instead nervously announced her presence. "Hello, Charlie is it?"

"Yes it is Ma'am." Charlie answered. He was surprised but didn't let on as he turned to face her with an aura of confidence seemed to create a glow around him.

"Well I'm Mrs. Johnson the lady of the house. It appears that

Lucille will be just a little longer and I was wondering if you would like to wait in the parlor out of this hot humid air."

"Why I'd be much obliged," Charlie replied while tipping his hat and smiling.

Mrs. Johnson was blushing as she led the way back into the house. She was giddy as a schoolgirl on her first date.

They entered through the servant's door and as Charlie passed Honey he winked his eye and smiled slyly. Mrs. Johnson ordered Honey to bring some water as if Charlie was her guest. Lucille brought in two glasses and a pitcher of water. She could tell by the way Mrs. Johnson, was staring at Charlie in fascination that she was ripe for the picking. Charlie began telling her about his travels to France, Italy, London and Greece. Every now and then he would speak a little French and it wasn't long before they were holding an all out conversation in French. Mrs. Johnson was well educated and had come from a cultured society family.

Mr. Johnson was a self made man unrefined and uneducated in the classical sense. He had married Mrs. Johnson in order to gain greater acceptance in the Delta's high societal circle but always felt out of place and unwelcome. He responded by alienating himself. He preferred to spend time with the lower classes because they made him feel important. His wife's presence always served as a reminder of his true social status. He had come from poor white trash and in the eyes of the old money common wealth no amount of material gain could change that fact. His feelings in turn made Mrs. Johnson feel guilty and ashamed for being educated and cultured. It was truly refreshing talking with some one and being able to be herself.

"Would you like a glass of whiskey?" She asked Charlie.

"Well, now I don't mind if I do," he replied.

An hour had passed and Honey was peeking through a crack in the kitchen door. She could see Mrs. Johnson relaxing to the point where she was becoming a bit unraveled. Her hair was no longer tied neatly in a bun atop her head but flowed freely pass her shoulders. The top button of her dress was also undone and that straight back chair posture she was so proud of had become a slouch that was a cross between leaning back and lying down. She had intentionally placed herself in a compromising position and her body language spoke volumes about her desires. Charlie read every word that created each sentence and bore one paragraph after the other to build a thesis of despair, desire and longing. He knew exactly what Mrs. Johnson needed and he could give it to her. He would create a surreal adventure in a world of smoke and mirrors, by encouraging her to wield the power of her womanhood, while allowing the dangerous act of being with him to strike a blow of defiance against the white male establishment.

The talking and drinking went on for hours. Then it happened. She looked into Charlie's eyes and edged forward. He spoke back to her with his to make certain she understood that there was no going back and she answered with a kiss. It wasn't a wild violent kiss of passion fueled by anger and years of pint up frustration, but a slow deep and deliberate act that was calculating yet liberating. Charlie now knew exactly who and what he was dealing with. Mrs. Johnson was game but he refused to be a pawn. So he took her as if she was a common street-walker. He was careful not to temper his salacious sexual aggression because of presumptive barriers society had built around white women. He would do to her what white men had been doing to women of color since slavery; while their own delicate flowers wilted from lack of passion. The pedestal had become a prison that barred the fever of spontaneity muddling desire in mitigating ennui. Charlie knew that any lover's insecurity lies in the unknown. What could some one else give that they can't; and more relevant in Mrs. Johnson's case was; Why did Mr. Johnson find his mistress Adeline so desirable? Was it because she's a darky and they wield some special power when it comes to such matters? And is that why white men are driven to murderous rage if a white woman even ponders such an indiscretion?

Charlie knew that she'd dreamed that terrible dream all lovers have when their love has sought the affections of another lover. He knew that she had visualized her husband giving all of her pleasures and passion to another. He knew that Mr. Johnson had withheld in order not to appear depraved in his wife's eyes and Charlie also knew that she had not made her desires known to preserve her Christian virtue. These truths he would use as his weapons. As Mrs. Johnson lay writhing and sprawled out in the middle of the parlor room floor he knew that he had given her the most addictive feeling in the world; the pleasure of freedom.

X
SUITORS

oney had been peering through the door but had stopped after she saw Mrs. Johnson's dress hit the floor. She then began to look out for Mr. Johnson as she and Charlie had discussed weeks earlier. Charlie had told her that if anyone comes stomp three times as hard as she could on the floor and drive off in the car as fast as she could. He had even taught her how to drive for that purpose alone. Charlie told her not to worry about him. He said, "If the war couldn't kill him for damn sure these country pecker-woods couldn't."

Honey had been waiting behind the bush outside the servant's entrance watching for Mr. Johnson even though Adeline had already told Charlie he would be at her place all night.

It was almost midnight when Charlie walked out of the door appearing a bit disheveled. His hair was out of place and his shirttail hung out. He was smiling like a chess cat.

"Let's go Honey," he said while refusing to take the car keys. "You drive darling."

Honey drove in silence to Paul Edward Street as she pulled up in front of the white two-story house her uncle began to prepare her for the next Monday. He told her that he left Mrs. Johnson without saying good bye and he knew that she would not know how to feel about that. He told Honey to play dumb. He also paid her twenty dollars.

"Uncle no!" she began to refuse. But after the look Charlie gave her she knew to accept.

"I'm trying to school you girl. Now you got bright eyes so I know you learn fast. Don't make me tell you again. For anything you give make sure you get and not no baby." He got out of the car and fixed his clothes. "I'm gon' tell Mama you been with me; she won't say nothing." Charlie took the keys from Honey and turned the lock.

Honey could hear the front door opening as if she was there but then she awakened to realize someone was at the door. She sluggishly awakened from her morphine-induced slumber. She usually awoke every day at this time because school would be letting out soon and one grandchild or another would stop by to see her. Today it was Nikki the second to the youngest. This one worried her; Honey thought she was too easy and the world would swallow her up whole. The look on Nikki's face often made Honey sad. It was the same look that all the children gave, one of helpless disbelief tempered by a newly found adult reserve that postured as if to say, "I will go through this with you."

But Honey had seen many before her meet the end and knew that no one could go through this with her, they could only stand beside her for this was the walk that everyone must take alone. It hurt Lucille to feel helpless but even more to need help. She had been the caretaker and backbone for many years now and she wondered who would pick up her yoke. The child before her invoked an undercurrent of fear that made the future seem perplexingly uneasy.

"Grandma, are you feeling alright?" Nikki asked.

"I'm okay baby," Honey replied. "How was school today?"

"It was good, Nikki answered."

Honey continued to look at her granddaughter's face searching for some semblance of strength, then went on to ask, "You have any work to do?"

"A little, said Nikki."

"Well you make sure you get your lesson." Lucille replied.

"Okay Grand Mamma. Do you need anything?"

"No baby I'm just gon' rest. Pumpkin said she comin' to give me my shot soon."

"Well I'm gon' mop the kitchen floor after I do my home work."

"I thank you baby."

"You welcome Grand Mama. Call me if you need anything." Nikki added as she left the room.

Honey did not return to her slumber but instead drifted off in a trance back to the past as she watched the haze of dusk smother the sun, making way for night.

As Charlie and Honey walked into the house her Grandmother was beaming with pride. He had the same effect on her that he had on all women. The difference here though was that he beamed right back at her. She was the only person he loved unconditionally. With her there were never any schemes or ulterior motives. It was evident that she was the love of his life. He placed her on a pedestal and would lay down his life for her with out giving it a second thought. He showered her with trinkets and money. He never wanted her to doubt his love. He made his adoration apparent and told her he loved her everyday before he left the house. Charlie knew that his father had used and disrespected her. And he felt a responsibility to right his wrongs and heal her wounds.

It was Saturday morning but all Lucille could think about was the coming night. She had not been over to Dockery Plantation since the night she and Tom made Verna. A great deal had changed since then. She was a woman now, with a modicum of sophistication, a learned understanding of human nature, armed with the uncanny ability to sense desires and intentions. She understood through Charlie's teachings that a man is always willing to give up something for what he wants. The trick is to find out what and how much. With her newfound income Honey had taken a stroll over to the shopping district on Issaquena Street to outfit herself head to toe. Tonight would be the beginning of a new life, one that she would control.

Honey smelled like a rose and looked like a vixen. She admired herself one last time in the mirror. The red dress she was wearing fit her body like a glove. She had a waist line you could tie a hair ribbon around, a bust line as firm and round as honeydew melon and the legs of a dancer.

"Mama I'm gon'." Honey called out. "I already gave Verna her bath and put her to bed."

Honey's Grandmother looked her up and down then gave her one long stare and asked, "Where you going with your face all painted, dressed like a Jezebel?"

Honey didn't want to argue so she ignored the comment and simply answered. "I'm going downtown."

"With who?" her grandmother asked.

"Myself." Honey retorted.

"Don't nothin', but a nasty alley cat walks the streets at night alone."

Honey knew her grandmother was trying to start an argument so she simply walked out the door.

The night air carried a gentle breeze and the sky reflected the luminous glow of a full moon. Lucille could see the crowd bustling about on Clarksdale's main drag, Issaquena Street. As she approached she noticed two familiar faces. It was Doll and her new Bo Paper T. Lucille had stayed mad at Doll for almost a year after she'd told Tom about her pregnancy. They eventually made up but there were still feelings of uneasiness. Honey placed all her trust in Doll and felt betrayed. She could never fully trust her cousin again and she grieved over the loss of her closest confidant because now she had no one to share her deepest secrets with. Doll also felt awkward and in fact Paper T spoke before she did. Doll felt guilty for telling Tom, but she also felt like she was looking out for Honey's welfare. Having a baby was serious business and she knew that Tom would marry Honey if he had known, but Doll never thought Lucille would be so stubborn that she would not accept. She had finally realized how different she and Honey were. Doll knew that if she were in that kind of trouble she would never bare it alone if she didn't have to. She would also go to any lengths to protect her honor and virtue and that included suffering a loveless marriage.

"Hey there Lucille," Paper T called out followed by a whistle. "You looking like one of them girls in the magazines."

"Thanks, Paper T." Honey responded.

"You sure do", Doll interjected. "That dress looks tailored made it fits you so well."

"It is." Honey answered.

"My goodness Honey, how can you afford such a thing?"

"I have my means." Honey smugly replied.

Men and women alike seemed to file by just to get a look at her in that red dress. Then Paper T came up with an idea.

"It seems that I have the two most beautiful women in the state of Mississippi in my company tonight, now that's a cause for celebration, let's go on over to Stovall Plantation. Muddy Waters and his boys will be down there playing tonight."

The girls looked at one another and smiled.

"I'm up for it, but how we gon' get there?" Lucille asked.

"Oh Honey." Doll interjected in a tone filled with pride. "Paper T just bought a car off of old man Canton. It ain't much but it runs."

Paper T then used his best servant's tip of the hat and bow, imitation; and in his most stately manner said, "My ladies your Chariot awaits." Lucille and Doll burst into a giggle as they followed Paper T's direction.

The ride to Stovall was a short jaunt by car but a lengthy trek by foot. There was no way Lucille could have made that hike by foot; especially not in the high heels she was wearing.

They arrived at Muddy's juke joint, which was nothing more than a cabin but the place was jumping. The music seemed to seduce nature and bring the night to its knees as one of its many concubines. Honey walked in ahead of Doll and Paper T; the room seemed to stand still as her presence created a melee of unspoken word; the men began to vie for her attention. She stood with authority and met her suitors with the poise of sage sensibility. Honey knew what she was looking for, but more importantly knew it was looking for her, and she could recognize it when she saw it. Paper T. pulled out chairs at the table so the lady's could sit. Honey then did something that shocked Doll. She pulled a cigarette from a golden case. The men were almost tripping over one another to light it for her. The strongest of the bunch cleared a path and said one word, "Light?" Honey made her eyes give a self assured, thank you. Then she crossed her legs seductively. Doll could not believe what she was seeing. She wondered when had her cousin become so sophisticated?

"So what's your name pretty lady?" The man asked.

"Lucille", Honey answered.

"Well my name is George." He stated as he touched the tip of his hat.

Lucille had sized him up during the scuffle for position to light her cigarette. She hoped he would win. He looked to be middle age but he was green. George was a farm boy and more likely than not a sharecropper. Honey figured that he wouldn't have much money but he could acquire some. The owners of the plantations where these farmers worked were willing to grant them small loans and supplies as long as they paid them back. The Negro men that worked these plots were tied to the farm until they paid off all of their debt or died trying.

George was a big man with strong shoulders and a serious face. He had been lonely a long time and was looking for a wife. He was wearing a jacket and tie with his button down shirt and overalls. Honey figured that the master of the plantation had given them to him for being such a hard worker and probably used him to be his eyes and ears while keeping the others in check. He was so used to stooping that he did it off the clock. It didn't matter if a person, were white or black if he felt inferior he would bow on introduction. Honey also understood that he was seeking status. He was the kind of man that valued stature more than things. But he felt that he needed to acquire the right things to gain respect.

"May I have a seat Ms. Lucille? He asked.

"Yes, you may." Honey answered.

"Well I must say, in all of my days, I have never seen a women as beautiful as you. Are you one of those black Indians women I hear folks speak of?"

Honey simply smiled; it was best to play coy with this type of man. He was gullible and would hang himself with his own tongue.

"I saw you as soon as you walked in the door. I thought to myself; that's my wife. Now, I know it don't seem right but it's true. I ain't ever seen you round here and by the way these men folks is acting, they ain't neither. I'm a real hard worker and I'll treat you good."

Lucille coyly replied, "I bet you will."

George was so happy his eyes seemed to be dancing.

The conversation was abruptly interrupted by a slender built Black French man. Gechie is what they called his type. His complexion was darker than Honey's, but his hair was mostly straight with a slight wave. His mustache was perfectly shaped and his nails manicured. He was well dressed but not in a flashy way. He wore a gray single button suit to match his white man's eyes of the same color, with a white shirt and black tie. His shoes were shined like a man trained by the military. In a word he was smooth. Honey found herself immediately attracted to him and this would be a major challenge for her.

She reminded herself of what Charlie had taught her and intended to make her requirements clear. This man was anything but gullible; he was worldly and confident. He would only be game if he wanted to. Now like all men, he had a plan and Honey's challenge if she chose to accept was to change it. Her uncle had told her to never try and change a man he's born with what ever is in him and you can't beat nature. What you can do though is change the plans he has in store. They made eye contact and the immediate attraction was evident.

"May I have this dance?" The man asked. George became incensed by the rude intrusion, but Honey put him at ease when she touched his hand as she asked him to go get her a drink. Then she answered, "Yes."

The gray eyed Gechie man grabbed her by the hand and kissed it as he led her to the dance floor. Doll could not believe her eyes and looked at Paper T in shock. Paper T threw back a shot of whiskey and beckoned Doll on to the dance floor.

The Gechie man moved like he was on stage. Honey was a pretty good dancer but he was a great dancer. He knew how to hold a woman, with a firm but gentle hand that guided, but never asked as they seemed to only make respectful requests. Honey felt that he could carry her in more than a literal sense, but emotionally and spiritually, spurring a different kind of growth that would take her to new heights. Honey was snapped back into reality as the smoky voice of Bessie Smith resonated in the background, she recalled how her song, "Down

Hearted Blues" had been her comfort at the lowest point of her life. She had vowed, "Never again!" Honey knew that if she were to act on her soul's notion this man would break her promise. She had to check her emotions at the door on this one.

"I'm sorry little darlin but you didn't tell me your name."

Honey answered, "You didn't ask my name."

"Let me offer my sincere apology." He continued to corn. "My mama raised me better than that. My name is Ezekiel, last name Flanoi but people call me Zeike. I hear your name is Lucille but some call you Honey."

Honey wondered how he knew so much about her and the expression on her face gave it away.

"I bet you wondering how I know. Well every man in the surrounding five counties has heard of a myth called Honey. I didn't believe you existed, but I knew who you were when I saw you. Now tomorrow I have to leave out on the Illinois Central but I'll be back in about a week or so. With your permission I would like to come and call on you."

"You don't know where I stay," Honey responded.

"Now that I've found you I know where you are." Zeke answered slyly.

Honey felt a chill and knew she was asking for trouble but she would enjoy it. George was standing by the table waiting for Lucille to return.

Zeke looked towards the table and teased, "After all that dancing, I'm sure you must be thirsty, I believe there is a drink waiting for you at the table." He then simply turned and walked out the door.

Honey immediately returned her attention to George who was happy to have it. As he pulled out the chair for her to sit down the waitress walked up with a fresh drink that had a note written on the napkin. It said, "I will carry thoughts of you with me to Chicago, Zeike."

XI
CONFIDANT, PARTNER, FRIEND

Charlie was shaving as he prepared for the day and to take Honey over to Mrs. Johnson's. He had been thinking about the old gal's state of mind, and hoped she wasn't too fragile. The one thing Charlie understood was insecurity. He knew that old lady Johnson would wonder if she had not satisfied him, if she was unattractive to him, or if she had done something to make herself less desirable to him. He also knew what would follow. She would first feel silly and ashamed; later she'd feel angry and hurt. It would be the latter emotional stated that would elicit the response Charlie would use to run his hustle. He knew that she would resort to using what she had to get what she wanted. She'd been given every possession she ever dreamed of since birth and though he was a man much more cultured and educated than her husband he knew that she thought of him as something less, perhaps a side show possession or a freak of nature. He would show himself to be anything but and sooner than later she would see him as a man.

On the ride over to the Johnson's he prepped Honey and reminded her of their conversation the previous Friday night. She was to behave the same as always and play dumb if Mrs. Johnson wanted to hint around the subject. Honey listened but her mind trailed off to her own hustle with George and fantasies of Zeke. Charlie pulled the car around to the service entrance and let Honey out. The routine would go as usual and he would return to take her over to the schoolhouse at noon.

Honey started her day at the Johnson's as she did each morning. She began by lighting the oven and stove. She then took out ham, bacon and eggs. Next she would begin to mead doe for biscuits and cook rice along with heavy gravy. Mrs. Johnson insisted that she prepared a large breakfast even though the three of them would be the only people eating. The man and lady of the house at the dinning room table and Honey in the kitchen. Sometimes Mrs. Johnson would be feeling lonely and she'd invite Honey in with her for a cup of tea. Honey hoped this would not be one of those mornings. Honey heard the sound of cowboy boots shuffling around on the hardwood floor. Her heart began to flutter. She had not anticipated the feeling of nervousness she felt at that moment. She suddenly became fearful that Mr. Johnson was on to what was going on. Honey's back was turned as she placed the biscuits in the oven. She could feel a breeze from the swinging door and thought for certain that death was eminent.

"Good morning Lucille!" The voice boomed.

"Good morning Mr. Johnson." Honey nervously replied.

"I was wondering if I could have a word with you."

"Why, certainly Mr. Johnson" Lucille answered in her best lowly slave imitation.

"I came in here the other night and was startled by what I found."

Honey became much more afraid as she noticed that Mr. Johnson's hands were behind his back. She remained silent as she looked over at the knife on the kitchen counter that was too far away. She wanted to run but the weight of her arms and legs seemed to be anchored by sandbags. Suddenly Mr. Johnson pulled a bottle from behind his back, the bottle was half empty.

"Do you know what this is Lucille?" Mr. Johnson asked.

"Why, no sir." Honey answered.

"Of course you don't. How could you? Mr. Johnson reasoned. "Well it's moonshine. And when I came in here on Friday night I found my wife sprawled out on the floor with this bottle lying next to her. She was drunk. Now I don't now how long this has been going on but we've got to help her. I need you to stick close and watch her. I have a feeling this has been going on for quite sometime. I have cleared the house of all liquor. I need you to tell me if you smell liquor on her breath, if she stumbles, passes out or takes a drink. We can't let anyone else know about this you here?"

"Yes Sir", Honey answered followed by a sigh of relief.

"Now I know you and the Mrs. are friends and nobody likes to spy on their friend but she needs you to help her and the only way you can is by telling me if she's drinking. I don't know where she's getting the stuff from but as god is my witness I will find out."

Honey knew that he would never find out, her Uncle Charlie would pay Mr. Johnson's mistress Adeline a visit and she would sabotage his investigation for a small fee of course. Mr. Johnson asked Honey if the biscuits were ready and told her to fix a plate for him. This was unusual since he rarely stayed for breakfast. Honey began to wonder if he planned to hang around the house more. If he did it would ruin everything. Lucille began serving breakfast and as she entered the dining room Mrs. Johnson avoided direct eye contact. She simply sat there with her head down, speaking in whispers whenever Honey asked her a question. Mr. Johnson sat at the table reading the morning paper. He finished his breakfast first and before he left the table he gave the Mrs. a look of disappointment and disapproval. He then turned to Honey who was clearing off the table and nodded his head as if to say, "You know what to do."

Then before the door could hit the frame Mrs. Johnson became a different person. She told Honey that she would need another bottle of medicine and asked her if she could ask Charlie to take her over to the round yard to get it. She then took off her robe unveiling a dress that lay somewhere between conservative yet revealing. It was obvious she was attempting to appear seductive and at the very least attractive, which was clearly a departure from her normal chastely prudent attire. Charlie would arrive in an hour and Mrs. Johnson asked Lucille to excuse her while she powdered her nose. Honey stood there in a state of shock but soon found her self laughing, until she cried. The old lady was crafty. Lucille had cleaned the kitchen and wrapped up the extras for an old friend of her from the fields. The girl was her age and already had seven children. Her parents had married her off at thirteen and when the first northern migration wave took place her husband went with it, he promised to come back for her and the kids, but six years had passed and no one had heard or seen of him since. As her friend was leaving carrying the small bundle of food Charlie was pulling up in his car. Honey greeted him as he inched closer. She clued him in on old lady Johnson's play acting skills. Charlie simply smiled. He would now begin playing hard to get. First he would use avoidance then he would play the scared Negro card. Finally in about a week he would give in to her blaming it on his uncontrollable desire and her irresistible beauty. He let Honey know that the plan had changed and now she would act as an intermediary. Mrs. Johnson was excited by her escapade and like all women would like to have a girlfriend to share her experience with. Honey would from here on out act as her counsel, best friend and nursemaid. Also after hearing about the conversation Honey had with Mr. Johnson that morning she along with Adeline would be in charge of keeping him distracted. He asked Honey if she understood the level of responsibility he was entrusting her with. He also made sure his niece knew just how high the stakes were, life and death.

Honey let Charlie know that she was all in but went further by asking if they were now partners.

"Now that's my girl, he chuckled. I taught you well. How does 70/30 sound to you? He offered."

"Well dear uncle seeing as how I stand to loose the same thing you do but I don't have to do as much 60/40 sounds a lot better." Honeys heart began to race just as soon as the words left her lips but she stood firm.

Charlie sat in silence for a minute but it seemed like forever. He had already taught her that when dealing in trade or money after an offer is made if you counter, never speak first or you will loose. Charlie burst out in laughter once again this time he repeatedly slapped the car's steering wheel. "I think I may have taught you a little too well baby girl, but it's a fair deal."

The games began as Charlie pulled off without saying a word to the old lady. Mrs. Johnson could hear the wheels rolling on the gravel drive and rushed from her bedroom out the servant's door. But it was too late. He was gone. She wondered if he had used her. She felt confused because she thought that they had made a connection. Mrs. Johnson also wondered if she had done something to become less attractive; was she not a good lover, was she too old though she was still a little less than a decade shy of Fifty. Charlie had ignited a fire in her that she had not felt since she was a young woman barely twenty. She was in Paris studying and met a young man from Spain that looked very similar to Charlie. He had an olive complexion with dark wavy hair and strong shoulders. She lost her virginity to him and in a fit of rebellion wrote her parents in hopes of never having to come home. The strategy backfired and her father had the American Ambassador to France arrange to have her sent home immediately and against her will if necessary. She and her lover were powerless. She was pulled from his arms crying and screaming, while he was dragged off in the opposite direction. She had often wondered what happened to him, though she had a good idea because the beating began before she lost sight of him. Her father never got over her indiscretion and thought of her as spoiled goods there after. That's why he allowed her to marry Thomas Johnson of no formal education or breeding. He was however a hard working man of the lower classes. Her father thought that it was the best that they could hope for under the circumstances. Mrs. Johnson stared off into the dust filled air created by the friction of tires on the gravel path and determined her self to not losing a second chance at knowing what passion feels like.

A few hours later Honey had returned only this time Charlie had let her out of the car at the edge of the drive and she walked the rest of the way. Mrs. Johnson heard the servant's door open and looked out the window in the parlor room but there was no sign of Charlie. She was sad and wanted a drink badly but Mr. Johnson had cleaned the house of all liquor. She paced the floor for hours, anxiously walking back and forth from the window to the kitchen door. Lucille was in the kitchen preparing dinner. Tonight would be another night of enough food prepared for four with a table set for two and a lonely woman dining alone. She was reminded of her husband's disinterest in her by the empty place setting at the head of the table. While the other four chairs, stood as a constant sign of her barren womb. Lucille began to bring out the first course. The tension between them was so thick you could cut it with a knife. By the time the fourth course came out Mrs. Johnson could not bare the awkward silence any longer.

"How are you this evening Lucille?" She asked.

"I'm mighty fine," Honey answered.

"I don't reckon you spoke with your uncle about last Friday night?" Mrs. Johnson inquired.

"No Ma'am," Honey answered.

Mrs. Johnson nervously continued with the conversation.

"Well, I swear I'm a little ashamed. I can't even remember what happened the other night. I guess the alcohol just got the best of me and I passed out. I've been meaning to speak to Charlie and beg his forgiveness if I did anything unbecoming of a lady."

"I'm quite certain that's not necessary. My uncle holds you with great respect, and as a matter of fact he sent a bottle of liquor over from the round yard to let you know that he enjoyed talking to you the other night."

Lucille sat the plate down in front of Mrs. Johnson and left only to immediately return with a bottle of moonshine. Honey could see Mrs. Johnson's eyes light up as she began salivating and licking her dry lips.

"I 'am a bit thirsty." Mrs. Johnson salivated, as she almost snatched the bottle from Lucille's hands and began pouring a glass. The old lady's eyes nudged Honey to go on with the conversation though there was nothing left to say so she decided to improvise.

"My uncle told me to tell you that he apologizes if he forgot his place the other night."

"Why, heavens no, Mrs. Johnson quickly interjected, but then she caught herself and attempted a more tempered response!"

"I enjoyed Charlie's company, I have never met a colored like him, it is simply fascinating, to see a person from such a lowly race of men speak so eloquently and French even; he is a true credit to his race."

Honey stared Mrs. Johnson dead on, and the old lady could tell that she had offended her.

"What race is that?" Honey asked.

"Well the colored race silly," Mrs. Johnson answered in an uncomfortable tone.

Honey's blood began to curl and things had now become personal. From that moment on the old lady embodied all well intentioned, arrogant, ignorant, insolent, liberal, forward thinking backward white folk, and she would pay their debt. Honey got pleasure out of seeing a white woman wallow in her own pity. Mrs. Johnson had been hitting the bottle hard all week and when Honey saw her last she was stumbling drunk. Being a good nursemaid Lucille had put her to bed and wiped her brow before she left. When she turned to dim the light Mrs. Johnson asked Honey why no body loved her.

Lucille replied "Jesus loves you," and left the room. The old girl was taking rejection hard and she was about ready to break. On the ride home Honey told Charlie about the latest developments and Charlie simply smiled devilishly. Honey knew that he would make his move soon.

XII
THE PUPPET MASTER

It was Saturday and the workweek had come and gone. Honey was bubbling with excitement, because Zeke had come back in town. He was true to his word, and had come calling for her. He brought flowers for Honey and her grandmother, and a baby-doll for Verna. Honey could tell that her grandmother was impressed, but she still held the hard line. He didn't stay long since he'd come by as soon as his train had pulled into town. Zeke needed to go by Mrs. James boarding house to get a room and freshen up. He and Honey made plans for a night out on the town later that evening.

Her mind had been on Zeke and George all day. She knew that Zeke was pleasure and George was business, but there were rules she had to live by and this would be her first true test. You could hear the music gritty and crisp, clear over in Durant that night. Eddie James House Jr. was performing at Smitty's Red Top Lounge that night. The place was jumping and Honey was having the time of her life with Zeke. He was well traveled and worldly. He twirled her around until she was dizzy. She had never known a man that could dance so well.

"Whew! Zeke", Honey labored through her breathing, as she fanned her face with her hand. "I need a break."

"Naw, Naw now Lucille," Zeke insisted as he pulled Honey to him. "We can slow down baby, but we can't stop."

His eyes were piercing and full of hunger. Lucille tried to avoid making direct eye contact but he stared until she was forced to and he made sure that she knew his intentions. He bought drink after drink, but Honey was a big girl now, and these watered down drinks were nothing compared to that round yard moonshine she was use to. She could hold her liquor as good as any man twice her size, but she played along with Zeke. House started playing his classic "Preachin' the Blues Part I & II". The song lay some were between heaven and hell creating an atmosphere that rivaled both the Pentecost and the Golden Calf. It took you to church while you wallowed in a din of inequity and sin. The rhythm was gospel but the guitar cried out in sorrow, lust, despair and hope. In a word it was organized confusion of which Lucifer is the master and everyone that came in contact with it was powerless to refuse. Bodies began to move and twist in unison with the agile perfection of a contortionist. Zeke made certain that his hands brushed up against parts of Lucille's body they were not suppose to but, she had desires too, and did not resist unless his hand rested past her lower back for more than a few beats. Lucille thought that if she'd considered for even a second allowing a complete stranger into her heart that it was time she allowed her cousin back in so she and Doll eventually made up though there were still feelings of uneasiness. Honey placed all her trust in Doll and felt betrayed. She could not get over the incredible grief she had suffered after the loss of her best friend. Everyone needs some one to share his or her deepest secrets with.

Lucille interrupted the barrage of words coming from Zeke's beautiful mouth by placing her index finger on his lips.

"I like you Zeke but I need you to understand. Around here you get as good as you give. You found my house today and knew about my daughter without my telling you, so I know you already know what it takes."

This time Honey stared him dead on and made sure that he made direct eye contact.

The evening had come to a close and Zeke escorted Honey home. He leaned forward for a kiss on the lip but Lucille offered her cheek. "You drive a hard bargain." Zeke said as he smiled and tipped his hat. "But I'm a man of determination." He said in his best Baptist preacher imitation as he winked his eye.

Honey didn't return his smile, but instead responded with a self-assured smirk. She felt her power and was proud of the way she expressed her womanhood with self –discipline, and self-respect.

It was Wednesday morning already and Mrs. Johnson had been pining for Charlie's attention since Monday. He had been playing the scared Negro for half a week now, but today he would be bold. When he dropped Honey off he was dressed to impress. He was wearing a double-breasted blue suit, with purple pin stripes, and a silk shirt of the same color, and a handkerchief to match. Charlie also wore a blue hat with a purple band, tilted to the right and broken brim in the front. The detail in his tie had a swirl pattern of blue and purple. Charlie's navy blue shoes were Italian made and spit shined until they deflected light like the chrome handle of a pistol. He was really dressed for an afternoon visit with a friend that he hoped would garner more leeway with the old lady. After Charlie brought Honey back to the Johnson's place to prepare dinner; he paid a visit to Madame Adeline to make certain Mr. Johnson would be detained this evening.

Charlie stood outside the old Victorian style, powder blue house that was trimmed in white, with a wrap around porch, and tall glass pane windows. During daylight hours you could never tell that a color woman owned this grand home nor would you have known that it was a brothel. He knocked on the door in a rhythmic fashion like the dapper chaps in picture movies. The lady of the house made him wait, as gentlemen should. The entire song and dance was merely a formality because she was no lady, and he was definitely no gentleman.

"Good morning, Mr. Charlie Wright. What brings you to my door this time of the morning?" Adeline greeted.

"Good mornin' to you sunshine, I must be dreaming or either I've died and gone to heaven. Because beautiful angels like you don't exist here on earth." Charlie took Adeline's hand, and brought it to his lips. He gently kissed it and brought a dozen roses from behind his back.

"For you my dear lady," He played on.

Adeline pulled him in by his tie and led him to her parlor room. Charlie followed though his eyes stayed fixed on her ample behind. She smelled like a cherry blossom and the silk robe she wore, tied at the waist was not diminished by a line or a wrinkle. She was naked. Adeline was a Creole woman with long red hair, and green cat eyes. It was hard for any man to hold his nature around her, and Charlie himself felt defenseless in her presence. Men in Clarksdale called her the cat lady because of her eyes, but it was also in the way she walked. It was even in the way she stood still. It was that thing that Charlie manufactured, but he knew it came naturally to her. She had learned from no one because she was the inventor, and the teacher. He knew why Mr. Johnson didn't want his wife any more, and in that instant he was reminded of why he had come by.

"I need to ask a favor of you darlin," Charlie requested.

"What favor is that?" Adeline asked.

"I need you to keep your Old Man Johnson busy all night tonight." Charlie replied.

"I see." Adeline responded as she put a cigarette to her lips.

Charlie was quick to light it and with the slight of his hand the match disappeared, as a green bill appeared its place. Adeline smiled as she accepted the offer by placing the money in her bosom.

"I appreciate it darlin," Charlie said as he turned to walk away.

"Are you sure that you don't want to stay for a little morning enjoyment?" Adeline asked.

"I'm not sure but I know better." Charlie answered.

The day had passed quickly and since it was harvest season the schools were closed. The cotton had to be picked by all, the decree had been ordered, by Mississippi's king. Honey had been at the Johnson's all day. The evening's sky of dusk and haze had smothered the sun, and Charlie would arrive soon. She could hear the tires turning on the gravel drive and so could Mrs. Johnson. The old lady was drunk and had summoned courage from a bottle. She had been pacing the floor for hours and mumbling to her self. Lucille knew tonight would be the night. Mrs. Johnson sauntered over to the swinging door that separated the parlor from the kitchen and asked Honey, "Is that your uncle?"

"Yes Ma'am", Lucille answered.

"Will you go and tell him that I want to talk to him?" The old lady demanded in a drunken stammer!

"Yes Ma'am." Honey replied in her best lowly servant's voice as she held back the laughter. Honey opened the door to the servant's entrance and waved Charlie in. He straightened his tie stomped out his cigarette and walked through the door as if he were the man of the house.

Mrs. Johnson turned around and was startled to see Charlie standing so close they were almost nose to nose.

"Did you call?" he asked in a low growl.

"Why yes," she replied in a startled voice. "I want to know why you have been avoiding me?" the old lady asked.

"Look I'm a colored man, and you a married white woman, my life is on the line." Charlie whispered forcefully.

"I know and I'm sorry," Mrs. Johnson panted as she sobbed. "But nobody has to know." She stated as she attempted to put Charlie at ease. "Look Ma'am you don't have to apologize and there is no guarantee that I won't get lynched behind this. You could die too. I just wish I didn't want you so much." Charlie stated in a pensive tone, as he turned and walked away, running his fingers through his hair to exhibit his frustration. When he turned to face the old lady his hair was out of place and his face looked distressed.

Mrs. Johnson could see that he appeared to have lost as much sleep as she had, and he was just as troubled. After a brief pause Charlie continued, "Look Mrs. Johnson we can't go on like this, we must end this thing today."

"Charlie, I swear I would never, ever let nothing happen to you," the old lady pleaded! She began to pull at Charlie's coat, gripping his lapels tightly. He forcefully wrenched himself away and turned to head out the door.

"PLEASE STOP!" Mrs. Johnson screamed,

"I LOVE YOU CHARLIE WRIGHT."

He could hardly keep himself from laughing, and Lucille was balled up on the kitchen floor, bursting at the seams from laughter, as tears crept past the corner of her eyes disappearing into her hairline. Charlie knew he had her and tonight she would become his woman. She would do what he wanted when he wanted. He turned around in dramatic fashion and took the old lady into his arms.

He kissed her passionately in between murmurs of, "God help us." This time he would not take her on the floor, but in her husband's bed. He carried her up the stairs, and at first she directed him to a guest bedroom.

"I don't like this room." Charlie stated firmly. "I need to lie in your bed and smell your scent, so that I can dream your dreams and know that I am your man."

Mrs. Johnson seemed a bit hesitant. That's when Charlie asked, "Do you love me?"

"Why, yes! Charlie, yes!" She panted.

He then kissed her with the theatrical flair of Earl Flynn and she complied this time without hesitation. The room was furnished with a king size bed that had a canopy top and baby dolls lying on the pillows. She was a little girl missing her daddy and her husband was not man enough to fill the void. Charlie could see that most of these relics where from her child hood, a time in her life that she longed for, it was a pity to see a woman nearly 60 years of age still clinging to such items. For wealthy people the bedroom tells you a great deal about their personality. The room told Charlie that Mr. Johnson was no man at all to have slept in a little girl's room. He was not even man enough to make her a woman. Charlie laid the old lady down and swept the baby dolls onto the floor. Then he took complete control. This time, he would make Mrs. Johnson commit. He commanded and demanded with a strong hand and a firm voice just as a father would. He made her, he pushed her and he forced her. He coerced her to do all the things her husband paid whores and field hands to do. He made her give what she desired until it hurt. He knew that it would please her to please him, as this was the nature of all women in love. She wanted so desperately to be used, and he would take until it broke her spirit or her bank account.

Mrs. Johnson for the first time truly felt that she was in over her head, but she had hungered for so long to feel that she was willing to settle for anything. The old lady was doing things that she'd been raised to believe were despicable. She also knew the kind of man Charlie was, with it being that he held no profession or proper occupation. She had already made up her mind to accept the terms of this arrangement. This man was simply powerful he made her beg and he made her crawl, she had screamed like a banshee and growled like a dog. It was half past eleven, and Charlie knew to be gone by midnight. Mrs. Johnson told him that she wanted to be the only one, and she could pay for that right. She had money that she'd inherited from her father and she rationalized her actions through those of her husband.

Honey had fallen asleep sitting in a kitchen chair when she felt a slight tug at her shoulder and awoke. Charlie was looking down at her smiling. "Let's go darlin'," he whispered.

Once again he let Honey keep the keys and drive home. As they began riding down the street Lucille could see her uncle dig deep into his pocket. He pulled out more money than she had ever seen in her life. "Honey Lump, girl we don' found gold at the end of the rainbow!" Charlie shouted. "Now I promised you 60/40 and that's what I'm gone give you." He counted out one hundred dollars in twenties, and placed the money in Lucille's hands. She was so excited that she had to pull the car over to make certain it was real. Charlie had shorted her by twenty dollars, but he planned to treat Honey out to a night on the town over in Helena, Arkansas at the Gambling boat.

XIII
NIGHT ON THE TOWN

Honey was all decked out in a black strapless dress, with a plunging neckline, and a white wrap. She was wearing three-inch heels, and a rhinestone necklace, with a matching bracelet, and earrings. Her dress was made of satin but she knew that these country Negroes had never been around anything, and they would think it was silk. She wouldn't tell them any better if asked either. Her hair was finger waved like the rich white girls in northern cities wore theirs. Charlie had left the house about an hour earlier to get some gas, and was still gone. Honey had begun to wonder if he were going to make good on his promise. Charlie often got derailed while out on errands, as he ran into people that needed favors or owed him money. He was the man that made things happen in the Delta underworld of the, a place where black and white mingled to create a gray social scene.

As Honey applied the finishing touches on her Madame C.J. Walker's make up she could hear Charlie calling from down stairs. "Honey, it's time to go girl; get on down here. As Honey began to descend the steps she could see her grandmother standing with

Charlie at the foot of the stairs. Honey knew that something was going on because her grandmother was smiling. "Honey," her grandmother began, "Charlie is gon' take you out with him tonight. I hope you act like the lady I raised you to be."

"Certainly Mama," Honey replied in the tone of a proper debutant.

Charlie opened the door and Honey blew Verna a kiss as she sat on the floor scribbling in a tablet. As soon a Honey hit the porch steps she could see why her grandmother was so pleased. Doll was waiting in the back seat with Paper T. Honey knew that tonight they would patch up their relationship and become best friends once again.

"There is your cousin, Honey," said Charlie. "I brought her along so that you all could stop speaking to one another like strangers. You girls are family and I expect for you all to act like it. You two grew up like sisters. Now it's time for you to start acting like it."

Honey felt a sense of relief. She had wanted her best friend back for a long time, but pride would not allow her to accept Doll back into her life completely. Charlie was giving her the perfect excuse to let Doll back in again and not appear weak. Charlie wasn't simply being the Good Samaritan his mother thought, he had ulterior motives, though he truly believed what he'd said to the girls. But he knew that just as the Johnson's needed a confidant so did Honey. Charlie didn't need her telling some lover their secrets in the throws of passion. Doll was family and would keep whatever Honey told her for fear of death. All black folks knew that if something involved white folks you better take it to the grave or get there early. Charlie also had side deals with Paper T and in fact, had helped him get his car through a numbers racket he had put together. He had other uses for Paper T and wanted to throw around a little cash to sell him on another moneymaking scheme that involved moonshine. As they reached the car Charlie told Doll to trade places with Paper T and opened the back passenger door so both ladies could ride in the back seat. He wanted the girls to make up and he wanted to discuss a little business with Paper T. Charlie started the car and revved up the engine to get everyone's attention.

"Ladies, tonight I will treat you to beautiful night of enchantment in the beautiful city of Helena home to riverboat gambling and the finest juke joint of them all *The Hole in the Wall,* where you will be privy to the delights, and sounds of the great Muddy Waters."

Honey and Doll began to clamor like schoolgirls and for a brief moment they forgot that there was any animosity between them. They gripped hands to signify their unity in the night to come. The moment became serious as Honey realized her forgotten grudge and tried to pull her hand away but Doll held on and began an apologetic diatribe that Charlie had coached her through.

"Honey," she started, "I just want to say I'm sorry for betraying your trust, but I was scared. I love you like a sister and you my best friend. I miss talking to you but more than that I miss laughing with you. Will you please forgive me?"

Honey had been staring at their hands held together by Doll's grip. She met Doll's eyes with her own and answered. "I will forgive you but I will never forget. You are my best friend and I will take all of your secrets to the grave. I'm shame of one thing though. I forgave Tom before I forgave you and he doesn't mean half as much as family."

About ten miles outside of Helena, Charlie turned up the radio; it was King Biscuit Time on KFFA. The nights show featured, "Howlin' Wolf". Every time Honey heard his voice it reminded her of a more innocent time, though four short years had only passed. She had not realized until that moment that she had forgiven Tom. It was more than just a forced prideful statement, but a heartfelt proclamation and she was truly ready to move on.

The car pulled into the parking area for riverboat gambling and four movie stars emerged. Honey Lump in her black dress with rind stones that sparkled like diamonds. She had a prominent nose;

fine and precise like that of royalty. It gave her an aura of wealth. While Doll, looked like a Persian Princess or a Lena Horne double. Paper T. simply cleaned up well. He was handsome with a strong jaw line. His eyes were deep-set and his facial features were keen like that of a Dominican or Haitian. He wore his mustache heavy and his skin glowed like the orange in a sunset on a late autumn eve. Paper T is what you would call a little big person. He was of average size but of a build that was broad, muscular and long. He was a country boy at heart and wore cowboy boots with his suit.

"Paper T," Charlie joked, "You gon' wrestle down a hog in here tonight?"

"What you talking bout' Charlie? Paper T replied."

"I'm talking about those old cowboy boots you wearin' with that three piece suit."

They all looked down at Paper T's feet and started laughing, Paper T. included.

Hanging out with Charlie took everything to the next level. He rolled sevens and elevens for an hour straight on the crap table. Then the house decided to conveniently shut down the table. They were sending a message and they all took the hint. That was just fine by Charlie he had won big and was ready to party hard. When they arrived at the *Hole in the Wall* they were treated like royalty. Everybody in the place knew Charlie and the waitress walked over to a table that seemed to belong to him with his drink, a scotch on the rocks.

"What will your guest be having this evening Mr. Wright?" she asked.

"Scotch on the rocks for my man here and a bottle of champagne for the ladies." Charlie ordered.

The table they were seated at seemed to be perched on an elevated platform that provided the best seat in the house. Honey was mystified and wondered just how many lives did Charlie lead and who her uncle really was. Did he own this bar and some one else was acting as the front man? There was no way of telling but he got the respect of the mayor in there. Muddy Waters even called Charlie up on stage before he started his second set and announced his presence. Charlie in turn introduced the crowd to his guests and let all the men know that Honey was his available niece for all "worthy" suitors to pursue. That's when things picked up. The suitors lined up like the Trail of Tears. Lucille coolly assessed and dismissed them one by one. Only the chosen few were allowed a dance, though the marriage proposals flowed as freely as the drinks. Muddy Waters then broke into his song "Hellhound on Mississippi." The night was simply a glimpse into the future of many more to come.

Honey rode up front with Charlie and the two lovebirds were sound asleep in the back seat. Honey had noticed Charlie paying special attention to a woman that looked like she could be Zeke's sister. She was Gechie for sure, black as coal with wavy hair and green eyes. She had a powerful build and a handsome face with strong features. By the way Charlie's body language interacted with hers they seemed to be partners and she certainly didn't defer to him. Honey had never seen him behave in such a manner around a woman. He wasn't charming or beguiling, nor was he condescending. The relationship seemed to be based upon a mutual respect.

"Uncle I don't mean to get in your business, but is that Gechie woman at the juke tonight, your woman?" Honey asked.

"Look here Honey I ain't got no woman, but if I was to have one she would be it. I knew her before I went into the Army, and she waited four years on me, with out a ring or the white man's validation of our understanding. But I always knew that if I had married a girl that black it would have killed mama."

After that Charlie looked straight ahead and Honey knew that their conversation was finished. They rode the rest of the way in silence.

Honey had been lying in her bed for about an hour, and was just beginning to rest when she heard her grandmother calling her name. At first she thought it was a dream, because she was saying, "Tom is here to see you!"

Honey hurried to get dressed and took the scarf that protected her finger waves away from around her head. As she descended the steps, there stood Tom in his Sunday best. He was still the most handsome devil in the Delta. Honey's knees wobbled a bit more with every step she took. "Good morning Honey," said Tom as he nervously fidgeted with the hat he held in his hands.

"Morning' Tom," Honey answered.

"I come by here this morning because, I been doing a lot of thinking," Tom began. "I just need you to hear me out. Verna is almost five, and I have done a lot of growing up in that time. Now Clarksdale is going to hell in a hand basket. The farming don' dried up and every man that can is going up north to get one of them good jobs they got up there. I'm going to New York and I want you and Verna to come with me. We can get married and leave next week. I still want to do right by you and the baby." Tom ended his monologue and waited on a response.

Honey knew her answer before the words left her lips. "No". She could hear her grandmother start wailing in the background. Tom looked a Honey and decided to take a measured tone to let Honey know the repercussion of her decision.

"I'm leaving next week and I won't be back. I would like for us to be a family but I won't ask again. Don't let your foolish pride get in the way."

"Look here Tom Knollins," Honey recoiled, in a tone that began calmly and soon swelled to a monsoon. "I don't need or want you to ask again. I have let the past be the past but, you have always acted like it was a sin for me to have pride. Is it because nigger women are so low they ought to be grateful for anything? Well I'll tell you what Tom Knollins you can just go ask your chittlen faced mammy to marry you, because I don't want you."

Honey's blood was boiling, and she had become engulfed by a rage that spewed flames like none Tom had ever seen. He stumbled over his own feet as he left the house with out saying goodbye to Verna. Honey knew in her heart that if he had only apologized like Doll and told her he loved her she may have given their relationship one more try. But there was no love he only wanted to do right. She felt ashamed to know that deep inside before that moment she still would have followed him anywhere, and all of this after the revelation of forgiveness she'd just had the night before. Honey knew that she had to have more. If she were going to live a life based on lies it had to be one she created, or at least be one that had been mutually agreed upon; with love as its binding tie.

XIV
THE OLD LADY

A few months had gone by and Honey was slow winding George. She didn't enjoy his company and knew that she could string him along until she needed him. Zeke however, was a whole other story. He was fascinating. He told Honey about Chicago, New York, and New Orleans. He talked about the South Side, Harlem, and the French Quarter. The places seemed so far away and Negro people lived like rich white folks. When he told her about the ballrooms and shops in Chicago she always followed with the question, "And these are Negroes you talkin' bout?"

He always laughed and said, "Yes, a lot of them darker than me."

When Zeke came to town they would spend hours in his room. He was a gentle sweet lover, and afterwards Honey would lie in his arms, while he stroked her back, and told stories about his travels. His words vividly described the scenes and transported Honey to the moment. She saw herself as a city girl, riding the trains, and standing amongst the tall buildings in a mink stow. The seed had been sown for her to leave Clarksdale. But first she had to save enough money and get over her fear of leaving home.

Several months had passed, and Lucille's Mondays began as usual. Charlie dropped her off at the Johnson's, and she had her secret meeting with Mr. Johnson to make certain Mrs. Johnson hadn't been hitting the bottle. She always reassured him that she wasn't, and he would leave not to return until the wee hours of the next morning. Once he left Mrs. Johnson would flutter around like a nymph in heat. Listening to what she called the great classics or civilized music, but it all sounded like a bunch of stiff white people, making a whole lot of polite racket to Honey. It wasn't that she was unfamiliar with the music or its composers, because during her early adolescence, Honey's grandmother had forced her to learn how to play the great classics by Beethoven, Bach and Chopin. Honey preferred to play soul stirring music like gospel or the blues, but her grandmother wouldn't hear of it. That's why Honey loved the juke joints, she went to have her soul stirred, and hear the band play sounds that personified pain, embodied joy and typified love, loss, life and struggle in the Delta.

Honey watched Mrs. Johnson carefully, and told Charlie that she behaved like a mad woman if he'd gone a week without seeing her. She drank heavily, and talked out of her head. Honey was fearful that she would tell Mr. Johnson. All week long Charlie had other business to take care of, no doubt these ventures had been bank rolled by the money they were getting from the old lady. Honey knew that their dealings with Mrs. Johnson would soon be coming to an end, but it was a delicate situation, and she often warned Charlie that they were sitting on a powder keg. Charlie had planned to spend some time with the old lady that evening, and she was fretting around like it was the Second Coming. For some reason Honey had a funny feeling that day. It made her nervous, and she didn't know why. She had prepared super, and cleaned the kitchen. She was waiting for Charlie to arrive. The sounds of French Composer Gorges Bizet could be heard as Mrs. Johnson twirled around the room, dancing with a bottle of moonshine, immersed in thoughts of her lover, but drowning in despair.

Charlie arrived looking as dashing as ever. He carried a single red rose between his teeth, a bottle of champagne in one arm, and a box of chocolates in the other. Honey felt that he was laying it on a bit thick since they had already discussed bringing the whole situation to an end soon.

Charlie and Mrs. Johnson had been upstairs for hours already when Honey heard a noise at the front of the house. She took the broomstick, and tapped the ceiling as hard as she could three times. Then she ran out the servant's door, and took off in Charlie's car. Honey was scared. She drove out to the intersection of high way 61 and 49, nervously pondering whether to run or not. She figured by this time Charlie was either dead or on his way to being lynched. It wouldn't take long for Mr. Johnson to connect the booze and Charlie back to Honey. She wished she had never helped Charlie run a scam on the old lady. It was foolish and dangerous, and it had cost Charlie his life, and she would probably lose hers. The whole family was in danger, because the nightriders might come out, and burn down her grandmother's house, while she slept. That meant the death of the only mother she had known, and her child. She knew then that she couldn't leave, and decided to head back home.

As she traveled down Paul Edward Street, a shadowy figure came in to view. Honey slowed the car. As she pulled in front of the house her uncle crept from behind the big oak tree. He was bleeding badly, and in the dark of night his blood soaked clothes looked as if they had been dipped in oil. Charlie hobbled as he rushed to the car, and told Honey to drive over to Helena. His breathing was labored, but he assured Honey that he would be all right. Honey was sobbing uncontrollably as guilt swallowed up her feelings of relief.

"Uncle I tried to warn you that somebody was coming. But I did what you told me, and then I left. I'm so sorry I left you. I wanted to go back but...."

Charlie interrupted her, "Look baby girl you did good. Don't worry your pretty little head bout' me. I'm just fine. A little banged up is all."

Honey began to rattle off questions faster than Charlie could answer them.

"What happened, Uncle?"

"Did Mr. Johnson do this to you?"

"How did you get away?"

"Slow down and I'll tell you." Charlie said in a weakened effort to stop the barrage of questions, Honey threw out at him. "I heard the thumps you hit on the ceiling through the floor, but the old lady was like a wild cat tonight, and it took me a minute to get loose from her. By that time the old man was making his way up the stairs, and he was moving fast. I heard him cock his rifle, and when the bedroom door flew open, I dove out the window through the glass and all. I got cut pretty bad, and I think I broke some ribs, but I'm okay. I know he didn't get a good look at me, and I think he was scared himself, because he didn't fire his gun until I was up and running. I don't even think he was trying to hit me. I think he fired it in the air." In a strange moment of reflection Charlie's tone turned sympathetic. "Ya, know Honey, sometimes a man can be so heart broken that he can't even fight." Charlie dozed off and it was left to Honey to find the *Hole in the Wall.*

Honey pulled up to the back of the juke joint and honked the horn. The little Gechie woman ran out quickly. She asked no questions nor did she speak. She grabbed Charlie and lifted him out of the car by herself. Honey was in a state of shock, but snapped out of it in time to help the little woman carry Charlie into a room hidden in the back. It was lavishly decorated. There were mirrors, satin sheets, Goose feathered pillows and a deep bathtub. Honey could see suits hanging in an armoire and a shaving razor along with a sharpening strap and reclining chair over by a sink. The women laid Charlie in the bed, and then ordered Honey to fetch some hot water and a towel. When Honey returned the woman had ripped off Charlie's shirt and was working on him like a doctor. Then Honey passed her the towel and she wiped his brow like a concerned lover. Honey could see tears well up in the woman's eyes and she became worried. The short stout woman grabbed Honey by her arm, and ushered her towards the door. In the light of dawn her face softened and Honey could see a glow of love all around her. Honey knew that this woman, and Charlie had been here before, and that she would love him back to life if she had to.

"You go on and leave now chile." She instructed Honey as she led her to the door. "Don't worry about a thing. I will take good care of him now."

Honey rushed back to the Johnson's house as the sun rose. She was careful to park Charlie's car out of sight. She cooked breakfast like usual, and waited to see her fate. Old man Johnson was the only one to come down that morning. He said nothing to Honey, and only drank a cup of coffee before he left. He looked like a man whose world had come to an end. He was too numb to feel. Honey felt a sense of relief in his silence. When he left Honey's friend from the fields came to the servant's door for leftovers. Honey pulled the girl close, and told her to get word to her Mama that she was fine, and would be home at noon. The girl promised to send one of her boys over to pass along the message. Honey then proceeded up the stairs to Mrs. Johnson's bedroom. She could hear muffled cries. Honey knocked in a whisper twice.

"Lucille, is that you?" Mrs. Johnson asked in a contrived, controlled tone.

"Yes Ma'am," Honey answered.

"Come in my dear friend." The old lady pleaded.

Lucille eased open the door, but was not ready for what she saw. The prim and proper woman had become a disheveled wreck. She had been an older lady that had aged well, but now she was an old woman. The neatly tied bun that once sat atop her head had become a wild, matted, and mangled mess that personified the distress lines that met wrinkles from age, to make her an elderly woman over night. Honey knew that Mrs. Johnson was headed to the infirmary or permanent bed rest. She noticed bottles of pills sitting on the night stand. And she could tell by the way the old lady rocked back and forth, while hugging her knees, that she was headed for a nervous break down.

Mrs. Johnson reached out to Honey like an infant, and Honey took her into her arms, as the old lady told her that her father wouldn't let her see Alejandro anymore, and that she wanted to die. The old lady never mentioned Charlie, but wept and cried incessantly for Alejandro. He was the Spanish boy she'd loved so many years ago in France. Lucille couldn't make any sense out of what she was saying, and just as she was about to ask the old lady if she'd remembered anything about the last seven months. In walked Mr. Johnson and Dr. Faggon with his black bag of tricks.

"Will you excuse us Lucille?" Mr. Johnson announced rather than asked.

"Yes sir," Honey replied in her best lowly slave voice.

"By the way Lucille," the old man went on before she left the room. "Would you mind waiting down stairs just a moment before you leave?"

"Why, certainly sir." Honey answered with a bowed head as she eased out the door.

Honey waited in the kitchen fearful of what might happen next. Her mind was turning over thoughts and scenarios too numerous to measure by time or count as they all ran together in a mirage of panic and trepidation. As the swinging doors crept, open Honey could feel beads of sweat stream down her back. She wiped her brow incessantly as she prayed for a quick death, and doubted her decision not to run. The first thing she saw was Mr. Johnson's boots; they had never appeared so big before. He seemed to be leaning into the door more so than pushing it open. When he finally revealed himself the boots he was wearing seemed to dwarf him. He almost crumpled to the floor like a man whose very soul had been weighted down by a sack of bricks. Honey stepped forward to help brace him before he fell. He sought the comfort of refuge on her bosom, as he began to cry an uncontrollable cry, the kind of cry were your body shakes, and your head pounds until your eyes are blood shot red and though your chest heaves up and down your body refuses to draw breath. He was a man suffering from a great loss and he grieved openly. After more time had passed than Honey felt comfortable, having this white mans head on her breast, he began to speak.

"Lucille I want to thank you for all you have done for my wife. You have been a nursemaid and a friend. I truly appreciate it. The doctor said she gone now outta her mind. She's been talkin' outta her head all day. I think this has been coming to pass for quite some time now, and she tried to fight it with the alcohol. I don't know what brought this on."

Honey removed her hand from his shoulder, as he lied. She became sick to her stomach. He knew exactly what brought on her current state of mind. But in order to save face he was willing to sacrifice his wife's sanity. He didn't know if the man that jumped from their bedroom window the night before was a lover or a rapist, and he didn't care to know.

Old man Johnson looked Honey in the eyes as he placed a fairly hefty severance in her hand. "I'm sorry for such short notice, but we won't be needing your services any longer. The doctor said that there ain't much we can do for her here, and that she needs to be under the care of a head doctor. We gon' drive her over to Jackson tonight."

Mr. Johnson wiped his face and stood up from the chair as he left the kitchen without giving any further direction or saying good bye. Honey ran all the way to Charlie's car and drove to her grandmother's house on Paul Edward Street, in a daze. She ignored her grandmother's questions as she filled the tub for a bath. She must have soaked and scrubbed for what seemed like all day, as the sun began its descent. She tried to get rid of the dirt that stained her soul, but she knew in her heart that she would never be able to. The day had taught her a valuable lesson and now she had developed a skill set under Charlie's tutelage that she could implore with the shrewd sensibility of a sage veteran. Honey, thought to herself as she rose from the tub; people will throw you away like yesterday's paper and then murmured what her grandmother had always told her, "Don't know body love you but Jesus."

XV
GEORGE

Two weeks had gone by and Charlie had returned home. He seemed a bit distant, and Honey wondered if she had done something wrong. She had not been to see him during his recuperation, but that was what he had told her to do. He was afraid that she would lead some one to him. As it turned out no one was looking for the black man that jumped from the window; Mr. Johnson was probably too ashamed. The old lady had been sent to an insane asylum and would probably never live to tell the truth. Honey was happy that it was all over, but had been seduced by the easy money, and had begun contemplating her next move. She knew that the harvest would be coming soon and decided that it was time to make old George the sharecropper pay for all the company she had been keeping him. He had always treated her nice and she never left empty handed, but what she wanted was some real money. She had almost become accustom to the income she and Charlie derived from Old Lady Johnson. She was now without a job and no under the table income, but the harvest was coming.

The tenant's quarters over at Dockery Plantation had been jumping all week long as the harvest was coming to an end. Everyone who was somebody played there. It seemed that on any given night you could see Robert Johnson, Howlin Wolf, Bessie Smith or a young John Hooker. The money, moonshine, and lovin' flowed freely. Honey partook in everything except the lovin'. George never pressed her, either. His intentions were true. He intended to make an honest woman of Honey. She on the other hand had no intentions of marrying him or anyone else in Clarksdale.

The Delta's air seemed to be getting thinner these days and she knew that it would suffocate her spirit if she didn't leave soon. There had been times when she actually felt sorry for George and appreciated the fact that he thought so highly of her. But George was tight with his money. She had given him a few kisses, and even let him feel her up, but he only came up with twenty dollars. Honey had him figured though and knew what it would take to get her hands on his piggy bank. George had asked about Verna several times, and talked all the time about them becoming a family, and him making an honest woman out of Honey. He'd promised to be a good husband to Honey, and a real father to Verna. Honey had decided to play on his need to save and make whole. She noticed how gentle and caring he was with the children on the plantation. He had also told her that he wanted a large family, because as he put it, "Children are the only innocent creatures that walk the lords green earth."

He also told Honey that he knew how to make money share cropping, and had done so for four years in a row now. He said that he talks to the white man like he don't have any other ambitions, but to sharecrop, and he didn't mind being his eyes and ears. He told Honey that everything had been going according to plan, and that this was his last year on the plantation. He was looking to get married and had saved enough money to buy his own patch of land, and build a house too. So Honey knew there was money to be had with old George, and had finally figured out how to get it.

Honey danced closely with George all night and he felt like a king. She was wearing a white form fitting dress with silver shoes and rhinestone Jewelry. It was a bit much for the tenant's quarters, but for him to feel like royalty she had to look like a queen. His eyes seemed to dance with love as he stared into Honey's.

"Lucille," George began. "Have you given any more thought to what I asked you the other day?"

"Of course I have." She answered. "But... Honey hesitated."

"But, what?" George interjected.

"I'm not sure you know what you're getting into, Honey replied."

"I know you Lucille, and that's enough for me." George reassured.

Honey was smiling inside, because she knew she had him now. She began to tear up, and blink her eyes repeatedly.

"What's wrong Lucille?" George asked in his usual gullible tone. He was a prudent man, but too eager to please. It was not with intelligence that he had beaten the sharecropping system, but his sensibility. However, love had a way of making a person lose all discerning abilities. Honey bowed her head in a shameful manner and seemed to keep her head lowered as she raised those big brown eyes of hers.

"It's my daughter, Verna. She's a sickly child and she suffers from that breathing disease. I took her to all the local doctors, but none can help her. They told me she needs to go to Jackson or Memphis, but I don't have any money to pay a big city doctor. It's a hard thing to raise a sick child, but more than that it's sad and frightening. No mother wants to accept that they might have to bury their child. It's supposed to be the other way around."

"Why didn't you tell me Lucille?" George asked.

"Because I like you, and I didn't want to run you off. Most men hear about a sick baby and run the other way."

George wrapped his arms around Honey and hugged her firmly.

"I would never do that to you Lucille I want us to be a family. I'm gon' prove it by helping that baby get what she needs. So don't you worry your pretty little head about that now."

Honey could hardly breath he was holding her so tight.

Honey and Doll laughed all the way home, as they rode back from the plantation in Paper T's car. Honey told Doll about her plans for George and his money. She told her that she had asked him for a thousand dollars. He told her that he would have the money for her Monday morning and a little more if she needed it once all the crops came in. Monday had come and gone now the weekend was near. George had come through just like he promised, and Honey had made the mistake of thanking him with a promise she never intended to keep.

She was feeling like a woman of the world. She and her grandmother had an argument earlier in the week and Honey decided to move out and get a room. This was almost unheard of in the small town south during the 1940's. Girls stayed at home until they got married. Honey had received a telegram from Zeke and he knew where she would be once his train pulled into the Illinois Central station. He had decided to play sick and get dropped off in Clarksdale instead of going on to New Orleans, since this was not his usual weekend to come into town. He told Honey that he missed her and the feeling was mutual. She had never liked a dark skinned man before, but he was different.

He was confident and strong. He was well dressed and well spoken. Zeke was always impeccably groomed and his grey eyes seemed to peer into Honey's soul. He made powerful love and his hands were firm. He was a lover in every way. All the things that were said to be taboo he would partake in. Honey knew that she didn't love him, but she certainly lusted for him. He had shown and taught her things. Zeke made love to her mind as well as her body and treated her like an equal. He also understood Honeys motives, and obliged without her having to ask, as not to cheapen the time they spent together. He would always kiss her before he left and then he'd slip a few bills into her hand, as they stood on her grandmother's porch. Then he would tell her to go out and buy something pretty for the next time he saw her.

Honey heard a tap, tap, tap on the door and her heart sank into her stomach. She opened the door without asking who was there, and standing in front of her was the epitome of what it means to be tall dark and handsome. Zeke's skin was like rich dark chocolate and his eyes seemed to billowy like a smoky gray cloud as they hypnotize. He looked like an ancient Mediterranean prince. Though his complexion was enriched by melanin, the sun had left a scarlet glow that melded into lushes, waves of thick black curls. He was broad shouldered, but slim bodied, rippled with muscles yet long and lean. He moved like a cat and loved like a lion. He was the perfect human form that Michael Angelo failed to replicate with his statute of *David in Florence*.

"My Honey sweet Honey Dew how I've dreamed about lovin' you!" Zeke charmed as he took Honey into his arms, lifting her from the floor. Lucille loved the strength of his arms and felt petite in his presence though she was a well-endowed woman, with full hips, ample breasts and a backside that spherically matched the mathematical dimensions of 180 degrees circumference, causing the eyes of men to well with tears, like the stinging reaction produced by freshly cut onions. His love seemed to posses the power of the Holy Spirit, giving comfort and joy. Every encounter seemed to renew her faith, but like a Sunday morning sermon the message lost its hold as the days went on, and Honey was glad that he couldn't stay for long. The first night would be like all the other first nights; spent in bed.

Friday night seemed to run into Saturday night, and the two found themselves on Stovall Plantation in Muddy Waters juke joint. They were dancing at a slow winding pace, as their bodies melded together becoming one, you could hardly tell were he began and she ended. They stared into one another eyes with intentions that could not have been shouted more clearly.

Unbeknownst to Honey, George was sitting in a dark corner beside the bar viewing the entire scene. He was furious but not yet incensed with rage. He had been paralyzed by heartache and though he longed to call out in curses, his tongue had betrayed him. As he stared unable to blink, watching the couple walk out the door, a single tear rolled down his face as fire spew an invisible, venomous ray of vapors from his eyes that had formulated in the pit of his soul.

XVI
A CLOSE BRUSH

Lucille had been awake, but she lay still in silence, as she remembered a time she wished she could have bottled up. "Grand Mama, it's time to take your medicine now." The young girl prompted. She was a gentle spirit and Lucille thought that perhaps when the suffering became unbearable she would have mercy and help her to end it all. Nikki was second to the baby grand girl. She would cry if you looked at her wrong. Honey had been pushing her to be more assertive, and to fight back, or even curse in retaliation. She seemed to be coming along at times, but it was not second nature to her, yet. Lucille could not remember a time when she was not ready for a fight. Her motto was *whether it be man, woman or beast the bigger they are the harder they fall,* and she meant it.

Nikki then asked her grandmother a question that conjured up all sorts of memories. "Have you ever been to Chicago? That's where I want to live when I grow up."

Honey looked deathly serious as she told the meekest of her grandchildren, "Never move to Chicago baby, never. It ain't no place for a girl like you." The last of Honey's words trailed off as a

Morphine induced sleep rendered her helpless to relive the past.

It was Sunday, Honey had decided to see Zeke off at the train station, and then make the stroll over to her grandmother's house. The sky was so clear that the blue appeared indigo. There was a gentle breeze that blew in from the south muffling late summer's heat with early autumn's cool caress. Honey had seen many a young folk leave Clarksdale, headed to big cities, exciting places, and she wanted to leave too. She was tired of standing still while Zeke traveled the country. She had heard mention of cities like Los Angeles, Oakland, New Orleans, Memphis, St. Louis and New York. Zeke had discussed Chicago and described it like coloreds ran the city. He said that coloreds worked in all the major department stores, and some were even managers. He described the dance halls and clubs as if they where magical events of pageantry. Zeke had told her time and again that she did not belong in Clarksdale. He told her that the women in Chicago couldn't hold a candle to her. Honey had grown tired of watching other people make there exit while, she stood waving goodbye.

She walked along in a haze of serendipity brought on by the weekend's bliss and the Delta's recently agreeable whether. As she stood at her grandmother's porch steps she heard a rustling noise in the bushes. Honey proceeded to take another step when she was grabbed so tightly around the neck that she thought it was going to snap. It was George, she recognized his scent. He held a knife to her face with the sharp edge just under her eye.

"Look at here Bitch you think you smart don't you? You been, spending all my money on that nigger. Laying round in rooms like the whore you is. I should have treated you like the rotten goods you was.... lying about your bastard baby. You took what I paid for and gave it away free. Now I want all that I got coming to me and then some. You better be warming my bed tonight or they gone find your body cold in the morning."

Honey was so frightened that her whole body trembled. She felt powerless and knew in her heart that he was going to rape, torture and kill her. Then by the grace of God she could hear Doll's voice crying out. Honey was almost unconscious, but once her lungs filled with air from the deep gasps she took, she turned around swinging, but George had vanished.

The girls ran into the house and Honey was now angrily, pacing the floor in a fit of rage, while Doll cried and trembled hysterically. Their grandmother rushed from the kitchen into the sitting room, startled by all of the crying. She asked the girls what was going on and Honey simply stared at her wild eyed and tight lipped; but Doll blurted out the sequence of events, describing its details with vivid imagery. Honey's grandmother ran to the coat closet and grabbed her shotgun, as she began to load bullets into it; Bud entered the house.

"What in heavens are you doing Mama?" He shouted.

"I'm finsta kill that black nigger Honey Lump been slumin' around with. He showed up here tonight and put a knife to her throat. He threatening to kill her and she won't say why. I knew there was something wrong with that cat-eyed nigger. He comes round here bearing gifts and smiling like an old chess cat."

Before she could go on Honey interjected. "You need to stop talkin' bout what you know nothing about. It wasn't Zeke!"

"Well, who in the hell was it?" Bud demanded!

Honey stared at the wall in silence. Bud was getting ready to lay hands on Honey when Charlie walked in. He was clean as a broke dick dog.

"Why is everybody looking like somebody died?" Charlie questioned.

"Some nigger done came by here and pulled a knife on Honey Lump, say he gon' kill her." Bud informed Charlie.

"What nigger?" Charlie shouted.

"She ain't saying." The grandmother replied. "But I got these buck shots for his ass." She went on to state matter-of-factly.

Charlie looked at Honey then over at Doll who was trembling uncontrollably. "Come with me Honey." He ordered as he grabbed her by the arm. Charlie snatched Honey into the kitchen and pulled her to him tightly, while he whispered loudly into her face.

"Now, I'm only gon' ask you this one time. Who is this nigger that done come round here, upset my Mama, and scared my niece half to death?"

"I ain't scared!" Honey loudly retorted.

"I'm not talkin' bout you! What's the matter with you? Can't you see Doll out there bout to catch a fit, she so scared. But you don't think about nobody but yourself. Now I taught you a few things over these past few months but ain't none of my shit ever followed me home. Now you better answer my question girl or I will beat you like you stole something."

When the name left Honey's mouth it seemed as if her lips were moving in slow motion. Charlie knew exactly who George was, and he also knew that Honey had to leave town. His arms dropped limp at his side and his head hang low. He looked at Bud avoiding eye contact with the ladies partly from shame and partly from guilt.

"We gon' have to send Honey off somewhere." Charlie spoke in a whisper.

"Send her off some where?" Bud repeated in a tone of disbelief.

"Yes." Charlie answered firmly. "Honey don' got mixed up with the head nigger over there at Dockery Plantation. If he get his hands on her the law ain't gone do nothing, cause they got to protect that white man's interest first, and if we kill him we gone fry for messing with the white man's money. This middle of harvest."

"Whore," Honey's grandmother screamed as she charged at her with the butt of the rifle. Both Bud and Charlie grabbed her.

"Ain't no time for this!" Bud stated in a tone that froze the room. He then gave Charlie a look that could kill. Charlie was left speechless as he pulled his mother close in an effort to comfort her but it did as much for him.

Honey felt like she hadn't slept for weeks. At times her body was so racked with pain that exhaustion made her feel like salvation's mercy had taken her on to glory. Her dreams had begun to mix with reality, as the morphine allowed for a portal that served as the perfect conduit into past dimensions of existence.

HAPPY BIRTHDAY TO YOU! HAPPY BIRTHDAY TO YOU! HAPPY BIRTHDAY DEAR MAMA/GRANDMAMA! HAPPY 71ST BIRTHDAY TO YOU!

Honey smiled to mask the pain and mustered up the strength to laugh a little. The children danced around her bed while the grown ups laughed and talked. The one thing that Honey didn't like was when they talked about her as if she were a child, or as if she wasn't there. This normally came in the form of statements like, "Doesn't she look well? Or, How well has she been eating? And how is she dealing with the pain? No one seemed to address her or ask her anything. They simply touched her shoulder in pity and smiled politely in an effort to mask their own discomfort. Honey understood the sentiment though it made her angry.

But, then she thought, what do you say to some one whose days are numbered? What do you say to someone to whom the Doctor has said, "You have six months to live?" No one knows the day or the hour but, soon. Honey felt both alone and lonely. She could only remember feeling this way one time in her life. She closed her eyes and drifted off to a simpler time, but one that held its own complications.

XVII
WINDY CITY BLUES

$\mathbf{A}$s she rode the Illinois Railroad along train tracks that mimic the flow of what the Chippewa's called the great-river, Honey felt completely alone. She figured that this must have been much the same way her mother felt at the time of her birth. Disowned by her family for marrying outside of her race, there was no one there to comfort her through the pain, or share in the joy of god's grace and blessing; the birth of her baby girl. Then Honey decided to think positive. She had always wanted to leave Clarksdale, but of her own volition of course. She had envisioned a scene of tremendous self-pride while, bewilderment beset her grandmother and Tom. She dreamed of wearing a brown mink stow with matching hat, a Carmel colored two-piece tweed suit, with a skirt that stopped just above the knee, brown leather gloves and high heel shoes complimented by a clutch bag of the same color and fabric. Her accessories would include a jewelry-set of gold, simple yet elegant; all these things the trappings of a wealthy, sophisticated, and worldly woman.

Things had definitely not gone the way she'd planned. Honey had to leave in the mist of dawn under the cloak of fear muffled by the whispers of tearful good byes. Her actions left everyone feeling diminished in some capacity. Honey's uncles felt powerless and her grandmother ashamed, while Verna simply looked confused and she was humiliated. Honey vowed to never run again and began from that moment onward to carry a straight razor; she would use it if she had to.

As she traveled aboard the Illinois Central Railroad, Honey would nod off occasionally and dream of tender moments spent with Zeke. She'd not had the chance to say goodbye or let him know of her whereabouts. She worried that perhaps George might try to take revenge against him in order to hurt her. Honey knew that Zeke could hold his own, but the element of surprise does provide its advantages. Tears streamed down her face as she became overcome with guilt, and worry. She had been so selfish that she'd allowed her own den of smoke and mirrors to prove her newfound wisdom false. In the face of her disillusionment it seemed that others would pay the heftiest bounty.

After the train had made its Memphis stop, Honey felt as if she could see the shore of her past in the distance, as she continued on what to her was paramount to the transatlantic crossing. She was headed to the land of milk and honey, Chicago.

Honey cleared her throat as she awoke to the comfort of darkness. The night was still and peaceful, but she was not alone.

"Grand Mama, you all right?" It was her granddaughter, Nikki.

"I'm fine." Honey answered.

"Are you in any pain? It's almost time for your medicine." The child spoke, with uneasiness to her voice, and Honey patted her hand to calm her spirit.

"You know Grand Mama ain't gon' be around for long." Honey stated, in an eerie tone of disconnect. The child tried to muster as much confidence as a gangly, awkward thirteen-year old girl could as she unconvincingly rebuffed, in a panned voice of practice that Honey knew had to come from well meaning, yet still condescending grownups.

"You'll be here Grand Mama. The doctors don't always know."

Honey hoped she would grow in to a confident woman and squeezed her hand to acknowledge her attempt to comfort. Honey wanted to build this child to rise up and meet a purpose that was greater than the both of them, but she realized at that moment that she did not know much about this grandchild of hers as a person. Tonight she would get to know her.

"So", Honey began "What do you plan on doing when you grow up."

"I don't know." the young girl replied. "I thought about moving to Chicago and getting a good job, like a lawyer."

"Oh! No, Honey interjected." She thought of how easy this child was and could never see her growing skin thick enough to make in Chicago. "You don't ever want to move there." The young girl held on to her dreams of high rise living on Lake Shore Drive as she continued to tell her grandmother what she had not told any one else. Then in one abrupt phrase her Grandmother shut down.

"Never move to Chicago."

The young girl stopped mid sentence and began to wonder why her grandmother would say such a thing, but she dared not ask. Honey stare into the blackness of the room as a window to the past seemed to open.

Her Uncle Bud had decided days earlier to send her to his brother Adolf. Honey's Uncle Adolf owned and operated a funeral home on Chicago's South Side. He was married to Aunt Area and they had a daughter Margorie. Margorie was close in age to Honey so she hoped that she would have a running buddy right from the start. Honey didn't believe in mixing much with folks that weren't kin. So if her cousin was a square she would have to hip her. One aspect of Honey's dream about traveling to Chicago did come true. She had a bosom full of money and a suitcase packed with some of the finest store bought clothes from Memphis to New Orleans. The Pullman porter had informed her that she had less than an hour before the train would arrive at Central Station. He also offered to help her locate any friends or family she might be looking for. Honey informed him that she would be staying with family and that her, very over protective uncle would be waiting for her.

"Your Uncle Adolf will be at Central Station at the southern end of Grant Park waiting for you." She read verbatim from a piece of paper. So as to let the young man, know that it would be in his best interest to move along. The paper also went on to instruct Honey to stay put and her uncle would find her but he would be waiting for her when the train arrived. She had also written down his name in capital letters, ADOLF WRIGHT as well as the name of his business, WRIGHT'S FUNERAL HOME. Honey figured that if something were to happen, where there was some sort of miscommunication almost any black would know where to find the funeral home. Things up north were suppose to be different, but Honey knew they weren't so different that blacks and whites shared the same funeral homes.

Honey stepped down from the train car and into her new life. She could see in the near distance her Uncle Adolf and Aunt Area, standing beside the two was a silhouette that she could hardly make out but it was the figure of a young woman.

"Hun Lump! Hun Lump! Over here Hun Lump!" Her uncle shouted out. Honey began to walk quickly into arms that enveloped her with warmth and understanding. She had wondered if there would be an aura of Wright dignified self-righteousness and pity or pure disgust. She was pleasantly surprised to find neither, only love and understanding could be found in her uncle's embrace. Her Aunt Area seconded the feeling as she squeezed Honey's hand and kissed her cheek. Then it was Magorie's turn to greet her, "Oh, Honey I can't believe you're here this is going to be fantastic! I can't wait to show you the city. And ooh, girl where did you get those shoes?"

Honey couldn't get a word in edge wise so she took in as much as she could with her eyes. The train station was beautiful. There were blacks working everywhere moving and directing the sea of passengers. Honey was glad that she didn't look like most of the

Negroes coming north for the first time. You could see the farm yard written all over most of them. While the Chicago Negroes looked sophisticated and regal, even in their work uniforms. There was something about the way they walked, like free men. Honey's uncle had aged a bit but seemed to only grow more distinguished. He was a tall man unlike her Uncle Bud with a frame more solid than Charlie's, he looked like the older brother and he was handsome as all the Wright men were. He had an olive complexion and jet black hair that lay straight with a slight curl on the end. He carried himself like a dignified businessman. He wore a long gray trench coat and a simple but elegant single button black suit. He was the total opposite of Charlie but dapper just the same.

His wife Aunt Area was the perfect accessory. Uncle Adolf had class and he allowed his wife to adorn all the trappings of his success. She was dressed from head to toe, wearing a fur hat and wrap like Honey had always dreamed of. She still had the waistline of a twenty-year old girl with the posture of a refined lady. Her teeth looked like pearls as her eyes reflected the shimmer of the jewels that draped her neck and hung from her lobes. She wore long brown leather gloves with a Pall Mall cigarette between her fingers. The whole country was in a depression, but you would have never known it by how Aunt Area was dressed. Honey's cousin Margorie was a miniature version of her mother and anything but square. She had a bubbly personality and a graceful spirit. As a pair Honey and she would compliment one another perfectly, sort of like sugar and spice.

The sign on the front of the building proudly proclaimed "Wright's Funeral Home" and business was booming because the powder keg of Chicago's south side living conditions made it ripe for murder and mayhem. Blacks that had been used to the spacious rural communities of the south now lived on top of one another packed into tenements like sardines in a can because of discriminatory housing policies that instituted segregation in de-facto terms. The south in many instances was like the wild, wild, west for most blacks and they carried that mentality with them to the north. Since there was no justice for them in the white mans courthouse they meted out their own justice in the streets, which resulted in profits for Wright's Funeral Home.

Honey Lump was a little scared as the car came to a stop in front of the all brick two- story building. She thought to her self. "I know they can't live on top of the funeral parlor. Then the car continued rolling into a turn that ended in the driveway, of a wooden two-story home. "Well, here we are Hun Lump." Her uncle proudly proclaimed. Honey could tell by looking at the house that he had made a success out of himself and since she shared the same blood as him she felt that all of her dreams would come true too. This was what she had been waiting for all of her life it was an opportunity of endless possibilities. In Clarksdale her fate seemed sealed. She drowned daily in the Delta's the destiny of murky the Mississippi's waters, her arms flailing as racism's strong undercurrent dragged her down. The northern air had resuscitated Honey's spirit and she breathed with ease. Now she would find her purpose and climb to the heights of what God had preordained as hers.

XVIII
RENEWAL

Honey awoke early as a force of habit. There were fresh towels lying on the bedroom bureau, Aunt Area had placed them there before she'd said good night. Then she let Honey know just how happy she was that she'd come to Chicago. Honey took a hot shower and dressed. She went down to the kitchen and began searching for ingredients. Honey knew that if she knew nothing at all she knew her way around a kitchen. She looked in the icebox and found eggs, pork chops and butter. Then she scoured the pantry for lard, seasoning, flour, and yeast. Honey felt her greatest since of peace during the early hours of the morning before dawn brought on the day. These were the times when she and the Lord spoke as she'd mead doe for biscuits. In the simplicity of preparing a meal for her family Honey found great joy and fulfillment the act was almost redemptive. A half an hour had passed and now the entire house smelled like fried pork chops and gravy, with home made biscuits, rice and eggs on the side permeated by the powerful aroma of fresh ground coffee beans. As Honey finished setting the table her hosts arrived just in time to take their place.

"Honey girl you gon' put me to shame," Aunt Area exclaimed!

"Em, Em, Em," Uncle Aldolf complimented, "It smells like down home up in here. I almost could have sworn that Mama had come to Chicago. She taught you well baby girl, she taught you well. And you a quick learner too."

Margorie seemed to stylishly saunter into the room. "Cousin you have put us poor city girls to shame. Everything looks and smells delicious."

"Let's say grace," Uncle Adolf interjected. They all joined hands and bowed their heads. Margorie squeezed Honey's hand tightly as they both fought off laughing at Uncle Adolf and his best Baptist preacher impersonation. They sat down to good food and conversation and it made them all forget about the time. Then Uncle Adolf came to his senses and began to scramble around in the midst of laughter's tears. Aunt Area rustled along behind him, as the speed of city life seemed to move the day along. Cousin Margorie asked Honey to spend the day with her. Honey was elated about seeing the city.

The girls rode the train over to 47th and South Parkway. The scene was like something out of a magazine. There were colored folks everywhere, looking important, not fetching and stooping. The South Center Department Store had Negroes selling its wares, running the cash registers and even managing some of the stores. The men tipped their hats as the ladies walked by. Honey quickly had a following as the catcalling whistles began and heads snapped as they turned around. There was a new girl in town and nothing like anything they had ever seen. She had country charm and city grit with a mind so fast she could out wit the serpent of Eden. Honey moved with the elegance of a thoroughbred and the gait of a jaguar. The reddish glow of her complexion gave off the aura of natures golden beauty as it is seen in an autumn sunset or a summer's sunrise. It was mesmerizing to all that'd seen her.

Margorie marveled at all of the attention though she'd notice how strikingly beautiful Honey was. Now Margorie was by no means any ones second best, but she had a slender elegant frame that politely begged ones pardon; while Honey was built to command an army of men, without the intricate dance of etiquette and formality. The girls giggled around every corner they turned with both of them knowing that interesting times lay ahead. Honey and Margorie spent the next few hours, window shopping and graciously accepting compliments. The girls rode the L home and Honey felt at that moment like she was here to stay. On the ride home she made plans in her head for the next morning. The first thing she had to do was find some work so for now playtime was over. Then she would get her own place and put to use all the things her Uncle Charlie had taught her. She knew the danger of the game she played and accepted its consequences. But she had sworn the day that she left Clarksdale to never track any dirt home again.

The next morning Honey did the same as the day before and prepared breakfast but this time she left before anyone came to eat. She walked the four blocks over to 25th Street and hopped on the L. Honey asked her fellow passengers where she could find good housekeeping work and was directed to the Lincoln Park neighborhood of Chicago. She exited the train and entered a fairytale. Honey had thought that Uncle Adolf had arrived but this was a whole other world. These homes made the Johnson's Victorian Mansion look like a shack. Honey was wearing the maid uniform that the old lady had given her. She planned to start working today and walked with determination. Honey would play mind tricks with herself when she needed to push for something, and she would usually imagine that Verna was at home hungry, and sick with fever and cold. Though she knew that Verna was safe and well at home in Clarksdale with her family it worked. Honey had walked past several homes as she noticed a maid or butler milling around, then she came to a home that sat still in the morning activity of caregivers and drivers. She walked up to the front door as she chanted in a whisper, "I can do all things through Christ who strengthens me."

Honey pressed the doorbell and within moments a small middle-aged Jewish woman appeared. She wore a beautifully plain dress whose material was so fine that any hint of embroidery would have only taken away from its elegance. Honey could also tell that the shoes she wore were European. This lady didn't have to stand in the doorway of a mansion for anyone to recognize that she was of considerable wealth and means.

"Good morning. May I help you dear? She asked Honey."

"Why yes, Ma am." Honey replied. "I'm new to the city, up from Mississippi and I'm looking for cooking and maid work."

"Well now it just so happens that I'm in need of some help around here. My last girl got her self into a bit of trouble and had to return to her family in Arkansas. Why, don't you come in so we can chat a while." Honey eased forward and humbly murmured, "Thank you Ma am." Once inside she could see just how wealthy these people were. There was a cherry-wood winding staircase, just off from the entrance and matching wooden floors for as far as the eye could see. A person could see there own image in the shine of the floors and Honey could see the reflection of her shoes. The home seemed quiet from the outside but with in there was a twister of activity.

"Oh, by the way my name is Ellen Rosenthal. What is yours?"

"My name is Lucille Ware."

"We'll then, pleased to meet you."

"No, the pleasure is all mines." Honey replied.

Honey followed Mrs. Rosenthal into a sparsely furnished room. The lady went on to inform Honey that she employed a wait staff of 17 employees which included gardeners, a butler, driver and several maids. At the moment however, she was in need of a cook. She asked Honey if she could prepare kosher meals. Honey answered yes, though she had never prepared a kosher meal herself, but she had heard from her grandmother talk of the old ways of life and how they had been raised in North Carolina. It had seemed that since leaving the Carolina's many of the old customs of their Jewish heritage had been lost, but Honey recalled vividly the things her grandmother had told her about cooking and housecleaning. She knew how to run a kosher kitchen and how to prepare meals in the old way her grandmother spoke of.

Mrs. Rosenthal asked Honey a few questions to make certain that she was qualified and then she hired her on the spot. Mrs. Rosenthal informed Honey that she only wanted the freshest food in her home, so Honey would have to go to the grocery and meat market daily. Honey would also be responsible for maintaining the entire kitchen. When Mrs. Rosenthal gave Honey a tour of the kitchen Honey was so excited that you would have thought it was hers to keep. The stove had ten gas ranges and there were two ovens. The best pots and pans hung from the ceiling on a rack and shined like silver and gold. The floors and counter tops were immaculately cleaned. Honey loved the smell of clean air and in this house it was everywhere.

During Honey's first day she did no work. The lady of the house insisted that she tour the grounds with her and meet the other help. Honey met the Driver Mr. Paul, who was an elderly man he'd worked for the Rosenthal's nearly thirty years. He had first worked for Mrs. Rosenthal's parents and now for her. Mr. Paul and Honey would become good friends because of their daily drive to the grocer. It was difficult to size up the others but Honey didn't feel that she would have to as long as she kept to herself. The next day was a new beginning and she couldn't wait to see what tomorrow would bring.

XIX
TELEGRAMS

T he rest of the week passed uneventfully. Honey was thankful that she only had to work the weekends that the Rosenthal's held dinner at their home and that was typically once a month. The Rosenthal's and their friends took turns hosting dinner parties for one another each Saturday. On their turn to host the party Honey would simply have to oversee the running of the kitchen. The parties were always catered, but she would have to clean the kitchen at the end of the night and that would be an awesome task. Luck was on her side though, and there would be three more weeks until her day of reckoning would arrive.

When she'd told her aunt and uncle about her new job they seemed a bit dismayed and asked her if she wanted to work for the family business or at one of the department stores. Marjorie even asked if she wanted to work over at the salon with her. Honey knew what they were hinting at, and it all came from that Wright pride, they were after all a bunch of uppity Negroes. Honey however, found peace in cleaning and cooking, it was a time of solitude when she could think and talk, to herself or to God. They didn't pressure her though and seemed to have a look on their face that said, "Poor child she still thinks she's in Mississippi. As soon as she realizes she's not she will come around and stop cleaning up after white folks."

When Friday evening arrived, Honey made her way past the Wright's Funeral Home sign. She trudged onward to the two-story home, that just a few weeks ago looked like a castle, but after being at the Rosenthal's all day it looked like something the white man had thrown away on his way to Lincoln Park. The entire street seemed to be littered with trash the rich had thrown out the windows of their fancy automobiles on their voyage to the land of wealth and privilege.

As soon as Honey entered the door Marjorie was standing in the foyer holding an envelope that read telegram. Honey instantly became nervous and wondered who would send her a telegram. She took the envelope from Margorie and read it. The telegram said, "In Chicago meet at G Park 12 pm. Z." Honey jumped up and down squeezing Margorie's hands tightly as she giggled with delight.

"What is it Honey?" Margorie exclaimed!

Honey shouted at the top of her lungs, "It's my man girl! It's my man!"

XX
TOGETHER AGAIN

Honey and Margorie spent the rest of the night laughing and talking. They dipped into Uncle Adolf's liquor cabinet to celebrate Zeke's arrival as they played tunes on the radio. Honey thought it was funny to hear music from two years ago being played in Chicago like it was new. She told Margorie about Dockery Plantation and how she had seen all the blues artists they loved so well, before they'd made it big up north. She also told Margorie about Tom Knollins and the man who ran her out of Clarksdale. She did not however, disclose any of the dealings she and Charlie had. Without Charlie in the picture Margorie thought that Honey was a mastermind. Honey used a slogan and life philosophy from the same speech Charlie had given her. "You don't even give a man conversation, and leave empty handed. If he wants anything more than that you make him pay his weight in gold, up front!"

She explained to Margorie how she and Zeke had a wonderful understanding and how he obliged her requests without bartering. Margorie could hear in Honey's voice that she wanted this relationship to grow in another direction. Magorie also knew that her cousin had to really like this man, because since the day of her arrival she had never mentioned him, and from her experience people only guard secrets that are near and dear to their hearts.

Margorie asked Honey if she could do her hair. She created the deepest finger waves that anyone on either side of the Mississippi had ever seen. She also dyed Honey's hair to match the red hues in her skin. Honey looked glamorous! That night Honey tied her hair down, and settled into bed as she tried to hurry away the night, with dreams of tomorrow's fulfillment, through tender moments of the past.

Honey was awakened by the suns tender kiss as it warmed the morning chill that preserved a sense of angst for the lovers of dreams. This morning however, she felt no self doubt but reassured by the affirmation of destiny. She and Zeke had a connection, that neither time nor space could transcend. She prepared breakfast for all and fluttered around the kitchen as she hummed. Honey was herself shocked by her reaction to Zeke's arrival and blushed, a little as she placed a plate of ham on the table.

Honey continued setting the table for breakfast, and soon everyone was joined together discussing the events and misfortunes of the past week, while expressing their hopes for the days to come. Uncle Adolf had two funerals that Saturday. He worked seven days a week because as he said, "People don't have the good sense to stop dying or getting them selves killed on the weekends." He was like all the Wright men though and seemed to be blessed with tireless energy. With a little trepidation Honey announced that she was expecting company that afternoon and asked if it would be okay. She was surprised by how quickly her aunt and uncle gave their consent.

They were impressed by Honey's courtesy and honesty, at first she thought it was because of the circumstances under which she had come to Chicago, but then they explained to her that most of the young folks had lost their good manners since coming up north. It was as if they'd packed up all of their belonging when they left the south, but left their upbringing behind in a forgotten suitcase. Uncle Adolf said that he would be away and looked very serious about wanting to meet this fellow, so he directed Aunt Area to stay home and size the boy up. There were no warnings about getting herself into trouble again, and it was refreshing to know that they seemed confident enough to trust that she had learned from the mistakes of a naïve little country girl, who was over taken by false charm and whispered lies, that promised unconditional love.

Margorie and Honey cleaned the kitchen and spent the rest of the morning preparing for Zeke's afternoon visit. Honey was wearing the suit she had dreamed she would leave Clarksdale in, a brown tweed two piece. Earlier that winter, she had nursed the Rosenthal's seven-month old baby back to health after he almost caught the death of pneumonia. The doctor had tried everything, and things were beginning to look grim when after listening to the baby cry and cough for days on end, Honey asked if she could care for the child. She used one of her grandmother's home remedies that involved a salve of live from a hog, turpentine and coal oil. Within three days the boy was like brand knew. He was crawling around and once again getting into everything. The Rosenthal's were so thankful that the *Mister of the House*, brought home four of the finest women suits made in the textile plant he owned, along with matching hats and shoes as gifts for Lucille at Christmas. When Honey looked at the stitching and craftsmanship of the details in every line of the suit's cut, she knew that these rags were right on par with what Hollywood starlets and the wives of wealthy prominent men wore. She thought about the Johnson's back home and assessed that in comparison to the Rosenthal's they never knew what class and culture was.

The Rosenthal's moved with a quiet, polite and dignified reserve. Material riches surrounded them, but you still had the feeling that they had so much more and wondered if perhaps they felt it impolite to flaunt it. Their lives seemed clean and full of life. Honey knew that the textile plants were similar to the fields of the plantation, but Mr. Rosenthal never brought the stench of labors sweat home with him like old man Johnson. He left the house every morning impeccably, elegant and returned in the same manner. There was never a wrinkle in a crease, nor a dirt-stained collar, or a ruffled necktie, and neither was there a mud scuffed shoe.

When Honey saw him she often thought of what her Uncle Bud used to say in that, "The lives of the truly enlightened appear seamless even as they toil." She clipped on her earring while checking her lipstick in the mirror, then the doorbell rang. Honey took a deep breath as she began to descend the stairs. Out of nowhere Marjorie appeared signaling for Honey to wait at the top of the stairs while she answered the door. She would greet Zeke and instruct him to wait in the foyer. Honey would then glide down the stairs as he watched a vision of loveliness enveloped his every sense.

Honey couldn't remember walking down the stairs as life breathed back into her body once Zeke held her in his embrace.

"Honey my sweet Honey; I thought I had lost you." He whispered.

Honey was awakened by a gentle touch on her shoulder. "Grand Mama it's time for your medicine." The little girl moved with the precision of a nurse as she pierced the bottled of morphine and drew out the medicine. She then held the needle up and flicked the syringe with the back of her index finger. As she pulled back the covers with respect and tenderness, the act became personal and loving.

"Grand Mama." Her granddaughter hesitantly called in the darkness. "Did you do everything that you wanted to do when you were younger?" There was a pause before Honey answered that rested on apprehension brought on by the pretense of not knowing what question would follow next. Honey answered, "Not everything, but most things for the times that I lived in." There were no more questions, but Honey felt a pain of concern. The inquiry seemed to foreshadow this child's restless spirit and the stirrings had begun, Honey thought to herself. Honey knew that her grandchild would need to get stronger if she planned to seek out fortune or fame in this world. She thought to herself that tales of big cities are riddled with the tragic endings of compassionate souls full of romanticism. In the silence of questions unasked, the past beckoned Honey to remember.

The showers of spring would sprout flowers of love that were planted in hope, and lighted by a promise that is forged on the bitter sweet release of a lover's passionate kiss. Honey now spent her every free moment with Zeke when he was in town, which was more often than not since they had cut back on his hours at the railroad. He'd been considering taking a job at one of the local foundries. It always made Honey smile on the inside when he took to such talk because she wanted him with her all the time. Lately Zeke had been talking about making things permanent. Honey was spending more and more time at his flat on the weekends. It was just a one-room apartment but it felt like a castle when the two of them were there alone. Honey had taken to staying out all night, but her aunt and uncle didn't seem to notice. She knew that soon the subject would be broached and decided that it would be best to intervene on her own behalf.

Honey decided to go out and rent her own one bedroom flat near 47th street on the south side of town. The area was full of old dilapidated over crowded tenement buildings, but Honey was fortunate enough to move into a building in much better condition. The rent was much more than she could afford, but when she went to look at one of the apartments it turned out that, the owner of the building recognized her from the Rosenthal's parties. He was in fact the Godfather of their son, and because Honey had been able to make the child well after the doctors had given up he rented the apartment to her for next to nothing, as long as she cleaned a few apartments, as they became vacant. The deal was too good to turn down so Honey had to break, the news to her aunt and uncle.

Marjorie already knew and had been helping Honey pick out furniture for her love nest. For three nights in a row Marjorie had kicked Honey's leg under to the table in an attempt to urge her on to tell, but Honey was too afraid. In Mississippi it was nearly a crime for an unmarried young woman to move out of her family's home until she was married. In Chicago though it was an everyday occurrence and more than that folks were living together in sin openly and having children too. Now the having babies' part was a bit much for Honey and though she could have moved into Zeke's shabby digs, she would feel more secure if he moved in with her. Besides, she knew that once she made the announcement her aunt and uncle would have to come and see the place. She did not need their approval, but she wanted it because without it the letters would start pouring in from home and she did not want the headache.

"I found my own place! Honey announced." The dinner table went silent.

"What do you mean? Uncle Adolph seemed to insist rather than ask.

Honey hesitantly responded, "Well I've decided that it is time for me to stand on my own two feet."

"Is this about that boy you been seeing?" Uncle Adolph began to pry.

"No Uncle!" Honey lied.

"Is it something we done?" Aunt Area questioned. "We hoped that you would feel like this is now your home too." She seemed to almost plead.

"I do feel like I'm at home living here and I'm so thankful to you all for taking me in, but I think it's time for me to stand on my own. I'm a grown woman with a child and though I'm not raising her I have to prepare a place for us to have our own space." Honey knew she was feeding them a load of bull but it seemed to be working, as both of their faces seemed to soften with a faint smile of pride and a hint of sadness.

"Okay," Uncle Adolph announced, "but we have to go see this place and if it is not up to snuff you have to come back home with us until you find one that is."

Honey knew that they would because the apartment was beautiful, it had hardwood floors and she had shined them until you could see your reflection. There was a fireplace in the sitting room and enough space for a dinette set in the corner. She had bought a red velvet sofa, and two plush golden arm chairs. To accent the place her tables were brass and glass along with all of the other fixtures in her place.

Honey had not left Clarksdale broke and destitute in fact she had made away with a small fortune between the scam they had run on old lady Johnson and her would be murderer, George. The furniture and all the fixings didn't set her back all that much since one of the yard men at the Rosenthal's put her in contact with his brother-in law who worked as a delivery man for a furniture store. Honey was able to acquire some furniture that had fallen off the back of a truck, but it amazed her that there wasn't any damage. Honey was clueless until Mr. Paul the driver at the Rosenthal's place clued her in on what it meant for something to "fall of the off the back of a truck." It served as a reminder to her that she had gained some street savvy, but still had the country on her. She would have to be mindful of that and move cautiously.

The next afternoon there was a lull in Uncle Adolf's day and he decided that it was time to check out Honey's apartment. As they traveled down 47th street the restless scene of cross traffic intermingled with armies of people marching in various columns, pursuing a multitude of objectives based on missions conjured up by an active imagination or as real as hungry children at home, who sleep six to a bed in an icebox of shelter where body heat is the only warmth they know.

Then it appeared as an oasis in a desert one lone four family flat. It was an all brick two-story structure that seemed misplaced. There were four cement steps that led to the entranceway and a solid Oak door that had an intercom which allowed tenants to buzz their guests in. It was rumored that the building once belonged to a mobster who had kept his mistress in one of the apartments and that was the reason for the buildings mint condition. Whatever the reason was Honey could see a smile come across Aunt Area's face and the frown rescind from Uncle Adolf's though he was not quite yet ready to give his stamp of approval. There was no elevator in the building so they had to climb two flights of stairs to get to the second story. Once inside the apartment Aunt Area seemed impressed by Honey's resourcefulness. She knew that the furniture was much too expensive to have been purchased in a furniture store and Aunt Area thought to herself that Honey had become a city girl over night.

"So! Aunt Area broke the ice. You girls have known about this apartment for quite some time. I love what you two have done with the place and I'm saying, *you two* because Marjorie is your partner in crime." The girls began to giggle.

Uncle Adolf was skeptical and for the first time reminded Honey of what'd brought her to Chicago. "Now, Honey," he began in a measured tone. "You know what chased you up north, right?"

"Yes, Uncle Adolf." Honey answered.

"All this stuff wouldn't be an indication of you being up to the same?" He questioned.

"No Uncle Adolf. A friend......"

"That's enough." Uncle Adolf interjected. "I'll take you at your word. You can spare me the details."

And just like that it was over, he never smiled or verbally gave his approval but Aunt Area smiled and nodded her head. Marjorie stood behind her mother and father about to burst with joy as she and Honey eyed one another trying to contain their excitement. Aunt Area turned to Marjorie and gave her a look that was playful though it also meant business, as she informed Marjorie that there was no way she was moving out of the house, and if that's what she thought she could forget about it.

The weekend arrived and Honey spent Friday and Saturday wrapped in Zeke's arms. He was impressed with her cooking and she enjoyed pleasing him inside and out. She wondered if he would ask her why she hadn't just moved into his flat but he didn't. Honey figured that after being in her apartment he knew why. It was Sunday morning and a distance seemed to grow between them as he prepared to head off to work. He would ride the rail from Chicago to New Orleans and though Honey often wondered if he had other girls in other cities he always gave her his weekends.

"Zeke," Honey chimed as she flirtatiously helped him tie his necktie. "When you get back, let's go dancing at the Savoy. We haven't been dancing more than once since I've been in Chicago. In Clarksdale we'd go to the juke every weekend. Now that we have a proper ballroom to appear as a lady and gentleman should we don't go."

"We don't go because it's not like Clarksdale. Chicago can be a dangerous city, Honey." Zeke stated rather matter-of-factly.

"You weren't talking about how dangerous Chicago is when you were telling me that I belonged in a city. You were going to take me to see the world. Well, I don't want to see the world. I just want to spend a night out on the town with my man."

Honey couldn't take it back once she had thrown it out there even though she and Zeke had never placed labels on one another before. Zeke didn't bat an eye. He simply put on his jacket grabbed his hat and halfheartedly kissed Honey on the cheek. She was mystified, but decided to brush it off as work troubles, with the rumblings of unionization, being a Pullman porter was becoming a hazardous line of work for a Negro.

Friday seemed to blow in with the wind and carried with it unseasonably warm weather for spring in Chicago. That morning just before dawn it seemed as if winters frost would strong arm the season as Honey was forced to pull her heavy wool coat close around the collar so that the lapels protected her ears from frost bite and her chest from a cold. As she returned that evening rushing to get dressed before Zeke arrived. Honey's coat hung loosely from her shoulders, like a careless child whose open book sack threatened to loose all of its contents as they ran home from school. It looked as if at any moment the contents of the coat would come spilling out and the sweat on Honey's brow indicated, she wouldn't have minded.

After climbing two flights of stairs she was met by disappointment in the form of a yellow and black letter taped to her door. Zeke had telegrammed that he would not make it home this weekend. He told Honey that he had to work over. He had worked over many times before but for some reason Honey had a strange and uneasy feeling. Wednesday had come and Honey had heard nothing further from Zeke so she stopped by her Uncle Adolph's to see if he had left any messages for her. She began to stop by every evening for almost three weeks for dinner in hopes of hearing news that he was all right, working, injured or even dead, she just wanted to hear something. Each evening though someone asked, how Zeke was doing or when could they expect him to join them for dinner. Honey held on to her secret torment and pretended that things were fine between her and Zeke.

Honey awoke to bright lights, tubes and the sanitized smell of a hospital. She was a little disoriented and couldn't remember how she got there. As her vision cleared there were smiles all around.

"Grand Mama is strong." She heard a male voice say. She turned her head in the direction of the sound but was disappointed by who was not standing there. Everyone was dressed in their, Sunday's best and the children carried Palm tree branches. Honey thought to herself that Easter would be here soon and it had been nearly a year since the doctor had given her six months. She only had to hold on a little while longer. The Morphine drip in her arm transcended the dimensions of time as the present was over taken by the past.

Zeke had been missing for nearly a month and Doll was the only one who knew the truth. Honey called Clarksdale regularly to check on Verna and to see how her grandmother and the rest of the family were doing. She had spoken with Doll several times and each time she asked her cousin to ask around about Zeke. Doll knew that Honey was very upset and worried about Zeke and even though her heart told her all that she needed to know love pressed on for faith in things not seen.

Another week was coming to a close and Honey dragged herself home from the L train stop. As she climbed the stairs she could hear music coming from her apartment. Honey quickened her step not knowing whether to slap or kiss Zeke once she opened the door. As her key turned the lock she heard low whispers and hushed giggles.

Surprise!

Out jumped Marjorie and Doll. It was spring break and Doll had earned enough money as a seamstress to travel north on the Illinois Central. She was coming to the end of her second year in College. Honey had almost forgotten how beautiful her cousin was and hadn't realized how much she'd missed her. All three girls ran into each others arms screaming in excitement and crying tears of joy as they held one another tightly.

XXI
LET THERE BE LIGHT

T he days and nights that followed were full of excitement.

It was a time of reminiscing for the girls as they told tales of the past and revealed their most closely guarded secrets. They had all now become women with tales similar to Honey's at Dockery Plantation the night Verna was conceived. Since Marjorie was in a very steady relationship her stories were not quite as interesting as the other girls were. Doll had surprisingly split with Paper T though he continued to pursue her from a distance while she attended Tougalou College in Mississippi. The most shocking secret that Doll revealed though was that she was having a clandestine affair with her English professor. He was the complete opposite of Paper T and his name was Franklin G. Gordon. He was an eloquent speaker and a beautiful writer of poetry and prose. He was slight of build with a complexion so fair that he could have moved north and passed for white. Doll thought that he held a striking resemblance to the young handsome Harlem, New York activist Adam Clayton Powell Jr. The girls squealed as they heard the details of the torrid affair.

Doll had herself, an older man but they carried on more like teenagers than adults in their encounters. They made love in the dark secrecy of parked cars, the couch in his office and at desperate times in her dorm room. There were no dinners or long strolls in the park. The Professor had told Doll that no one must know of their relationship or he would loose his position at the college. He always promised that one day they would dine with the leaders of the community and openly profess their love for one another, but that day could not arrive until Doll completed her studies. Honey wanted to tell her cousin to be careful but she thought to save the advice for later as not to spoil the moment. By the way that Marjorie's eyes met hers while Doll was speaking Honey knew that they were thinking the same thing.

Honey's affair with Zeke she thought was a true tale of lovers, which included all night lovemaking sessions inspired by wine and song, set in the backdrop of a small villa off the tip of France that was in actuality a one bedroom tenement on the overcrowded near south side of Chicago. Honey never revealed the current uncertain state of things between she and Zeke and had even lied earlier that week when she told Marjorie he had sent a telegram, stating he would do his best to make it home the coming weekend, and that he loved her. The laughter and storytelling went on until the wee hours of the morning. With Easter on the horizon the girls had made plans to go shopping the next day.

One thing about shopping on 47th Street was that you went looking like you had already bought everything in the stores. The girls were dressed from head to toe in colors that let everyone know that spring had arrived. They wore satin hats to match their crepe dresses. Which slung loose on the Caucasian figures seen in the Sears catalogue, but was given form and movement on the shapely bodies of southern beauties with breasts round as ripe melons, and behinds firm yet supple flowing into a waistline you could tie a shoelace around. Some said it was the food, others said it was the water, but what ever it was drove the men folk crazy. As the girls walked down 47th street, in and out of stores from the South Center Department store to smaller boutiques and jewelry shops they stopped traffic. They received a plethora of marriage proposals, and compliments that were flattering most of the time or lewdly whispered in voice and exaggerated physical expression at other times. The girls took their lead from Honey, walking with an air of confidence that matched the rulers of ancient kingdoms.

As they milled around the South Center Department Store Honey saw a sight that made her look twice and upon the second glance she felt as if she had been hit by a ton of bricks. There stood a lady with two little girls a few years younger than Verna. The woman was sizing up the children by placing hangers holding dresses under each girl's chin and then checking the length at the bottom. The girls were chocolate and beautiful just like their father who stood by watching with the pride of an adoring father. It was Zeke and Honey couldn't move nor could she speak. She just stood in a still of silence that drowned out the sounds of ringing registers, polite conversation and demanding customers in the busy department store. Marjorie and Doll turned around as they realized that their lead had fallen behind. As they turned their eyes saw the betrayal. Honey felt the eyes of her cousins on the back of her neck and pulled it together to put up a brave front as she blinked away the tears.

"Do you see that black bastard?" Honey spewed out with venom.

"Yea, we see him, Honey. What do you want to do?" Marjorie asked.

"Let's just leave." Doll reasoned.

"No I'm not gon' just leave his ass in peace. He ruined my day now I'm gon' ruin his." Honey seemed to growl as she glared in Zeke's direction. Doll and Marjorie began to follow Honey's lead as she headed toward Zeke.

"Hi, Zeke" Honey interrupted as he and the lady he was standing with were talking. Zeke turned around, and you would have thought he'd seen a ghost. He stood in silence as Honey introduced herself to the woman standing next to him.

"Hi, my name is Lucille and I'm Zeke's girl. Who are you?"

The woman retorted, "My name is Maybell and I'm Zeke's wife." She glanced down in an effort to one up Honey and said, "These here are our girls. Their father and I are Easter shopping for the family."

Honey could hear Marjorie and Doll in the background giving it to Zeke. "You ain't no damn good. You ain't no kind of man." Zeke could feel his whole world crashing all around him as he began to smother in his blanket of deceit. He was about to speak up when his wife beat him to the punch. She decided to be the bigger person by making her exit.

"Zeke, Maybell, announced." "I really like these two dresses here. I'll leave you to talk with your friends but I'll be waiting at the register."

Zeke gave a nod of shame in acknowledgment that said he'd be right over to pay for the dresses. He grabbed Honey by the forearms and pulled her close. Honey stared him directly in the eyes waiting for an explanation that could fix everything but there wasn't one coming.

"I'm sorry Honey. I wanted to tell you but every time I tried I just couldn't. I wish things could have been different."

Before Zeke could fix his mouth to say another word Honey slapped him flush with the palm of her hand. The sound that emanated the meeting of her hand with his face made heads turn and there was an immediate hush that fell upon everyone in the area. Maybell's head snapped around and she finally lost her cool as she flung the dresses to the floor and grabbed the children by the hand, she headed for the nearest exit. Zeke ran after his wife as security came running to ask Honey if she were all right. Honey coldly told them that she was fine as words from her Uncle Charlie flooded her mind. "Think like a man but act like a lady." She regained her composer and made up her mind to never make mention of Ezeikeil Flanoi again. Honey went cold for men from that moment on.

XXII
IN WITH THE NEW

In a few days things returned to normal as Doll traveled south again on the Illinois Central, but not before revealing a few facts about her college professor, like he was married and that she thought she might be pregnant. Honey told Doll to be strong because in the end everything would work out just fine. She also told her not to tell anyone else and to wait as long as possible to reveal her secret because once the baby was born everyone will shift their focus from her mistake to the innocent child.

Honey had decided that there was nothing like a new man, to make you forget about your old one and proceeded to look for a victim. She had not done more than get her feet wet in the year that she'd been in Chicago but now it was time for a full baptism. Honey knew exactly what she was looking for when she and Marjorie went out to the Savoy or Regal. She wanted a foolish man that had not yet quite gotten the farm off his back. One who thought being flashy and loud was a form of sophistication and he also needed the insecurity poor peoples everywhere had that made them feel guilty and ashamed for uncontrollable circumstances. These were the kind of men that had a tendency to brag on the things he had acquired since being up north and you would think that he owned the factory he worked for rather than labored in it. Her grandmother would call it "acting like you ain't use to nothing." This kind of man needed *things* to validate him so Honey decided that she would be one of those *things*. Uncle Charlie would tell her to *dress like you got a million dollars everyday because one day you might meet somebody with one, and they might want to give it to you.* This kind of man wouldn't have a million dollars but he would spend money like he did.

Honey knew that the real benefits were in the old rich white men she passed everyday as she traveled through the Rosenthal's neighborhood but she couldn't bring herself to violate the cost of freedom with a purchase that bought ones very soul. She had noticed the lingering stares that felt like sneers and perverted overtures, but Honey politely declined each advance.

"If you see a fool, bump his head for him baby girl." As soon as Honey saw Edmund James she heard her Uncle Charlie's in her head. He was as loud and brash as a man who had conquered the world. When in reality all he had done was leave the cotton fields of the south to pick up the north's yoke in a factory. Now the North did allow a black man some personal solace of pride and manhood but never equality in lifestyle or opportunity. Edmund was feeling his manhood living in the squalor of the south side tenements with a pocket full of cash. He was a flashy dresser but he walked as if he were still pushing a plow. His suit was loud and the brim of his hat had been broken like the straw ones worn by a cowboy in a rodeo. He had beautiful brown skin and a heavy mustache that matched his eyebrows. He was of average height with a stocky build. In fact Honey was taller than Edmund when she wore hills. He tried to carry himself like a big man but came off as a little man with a big mouth.

He saw Honey out the corner of his eye and the Arkansas, farm hand country in him let out a yelp. "Lordy, be what is it my eyes see?" Honey simply smiled coyly as she slipped through the crowd in a shroud of mystery. Edmund followed in hot pursuit. Honey found a quiet space at the end of the bar, sat on a stool and pulled a cigarette from a golden case. Edmund was right there with the flick of a lighter.

"My name is Edmund. What's yours pretty lady?"

"Lucille." Honey replied dryly.

"I can't recall seeing you around here." Edmund went on as he nervously felt around for an opening.

"That's because you haven't."

"Oh, so are you new in town?" Edmund inquired.

"No." Honey bluntly answered.

"Is this your first time at the Savoy?" Edmund continued to pry.

"No." Honey went on playfully wrapping him around her finger. "It's simply like you said. You can't recall seeing me. But I can recall seeing you." Honey was teasing with Edmund but he was falling for it.

He licked his lips in excitement. He was the kind of man who couldn't contain himself. He immediately bought Honey a drink and began telling her his life story. It turned out that he was from Prescott, Arkansas and had run away from his sharecropping debt. He was seven years older than Honey but seemed several years younger. Edmund informed Honey that he worked for a local foundry and made real good money. He was looking for someone he could spend it all on. Honey knew that this fool could be trying to run a game on her but she doubted it. There was an easy way to find out though. She simply had to make him show and prove. She would never challenge the lies he told about himself because that was how he built himself up. She would however make him produce anything that was in the material. Honey would take him up on any offer he made and asked until it hurt him to give. He thrived on being man enough and derived his manhood through his paycheck. He would work all the overtime he had to and even take up an extra job to prove that he was man enough for Honey. She would always wear her best when around him because he would always seek to introduce her to something better. Edmund was the perfect mark.

Their first date was spent at the Regal Theater listening to Fess Williams and his jazz band. The music was outstanding and the theater was glamorous. There was a sky blue canopy atop the ceiling that seemed to billow softly atop golden columns. The designers of the Regal used the best elements of the Orient, and Spanish cultures in their design of the structure. Honey was awe struck and for a brief moment wished that Zeke were there with her. It was just as he'd described it but better.

All night long Edmund spent money like it was water. He wanted so badly to be respected that he made himself look like a buffoon, buying round after round of drinks for some of the biggest numbers runners on the south side. These men made more money in a day than Edmund made in a month. Honey had met many of them before but knew that tangling with that kind of man would mean certain death. They all eyed her disrespectfully and Edmund pretended not to notice his "good friends" intentions. He stood with his head raised high and his chest out next to Honey all night long. He wouldn't even sit beside her but in order to draw attention to himself he stood next to her, showing off his most prized possession. Edmund worked long hours all week, most of his days in the foundry were 14 hour shifts. There were many nights when he would pull a double. All of this, he did in order to spend all that he earned on a good time. Every weekend he took Honey shopping. Then he would take her to the most happening super club, followed by a night out on 47th street.

Friday nights belonged to Honey and Marjorie. Honey decided that a little enterprising might do her some good, so she took to throwing after hours rent parties. They set a modest cover charge at the door. She and Marjorie would fry fish and chicken to sell as sandwiches to their guests. They would then sell beer and moonshine at five times the market rate. The business was pure profit. Edmund's money bought the food and booze, free tunes flowed over the radio waves and the rent for Honey's place was nearly nothing. Honey had no overhead and Edmund didn't know about her after hours' business because he worked all night long every Friday. Honey took the money that he gave her and turned it over ten times. All of the patrons were good people. She only allowed those who knew

Marjorie, herself or one of her coworkers. The atmosphere was always festive and friendly. The people drank until they couldn't drink any more and ate enough to bust wide open.

After her third party she spread the operation to include the vacant apartment across the hall. At the end of each night she and Marjorie cleaned up and left the place spotless. Marjorie was saving up enough to open a small beauty salon. She would rent out a space, and rent two chairs to her fellow hairdresser friends. Honey split the profits 60/40 since Marjorie had brought in over half the clientele and helped get things setup. She stored all the fish and chicken in the freezer at the funeral home. Then Marjorie had her boyfriend Bobby drive everything over to Honey's on Friday afternoons and set up the fryer on the back porch. Bobby also worked as security for free just so that he could make certain no one was trying to make time with his girl.

Honey Lump was fun loving, and the infectious party bug bit everyone that met her. She would laugh until she cried and danced until the last song was played. It seemed that she did all of those things while she performed as host and servant to her guests. On top of all that the men loved it when she smiled in their direction and when she walked in the other. Her hips had spread as she grew more into being a full-grown woman and her legs were as shapely as a purebred stallion. They were defined and strong yet soft, curvaceous and supple. Honey always played up a little to the ladies who came out so that they wouldn't feel threatened. People came from night clubs, home or directly from work. The atmosphere was laid back and pleasant, everyone enjoyed the down home feel. Honey let some of the guys play a card game or two while the house got its cut of the winnings. If some one got unruly over their losses Honey could handle a man as good as the next man. Anyone causing trouble was never allowed entrance again.

One Friday night Honey noticed a new guest sitting at the card table. He was rugged and hard with a serious face and piercing eyes but when he smiled you felt safe. His heavy voice boomed as he drowned out all of the other men at the card table. He talked more trash than the law allowed and brimmed with the confidence of a man who knew a secret that kept him one step ahead of everyone else. Lyle

Cook was normally not her type but he was a challenge and Honey liked a challenge. She also noticed that he was a winner and she was attracted to winners. It seemed that most Friday nights he took home the pot and settled up with Honey before leaving. Though he was the least handsome man Honey had ever dated he seemed to have a way about him. It was in his walk and the way he held his head high with a strong straight back. Lyle was a manly man but the one thing he had in common with the other men from Honeys past was that he could dress.

The first night Honey met him he was wearing a tan suit with a Dobbs hat to match. He was a very muscular man and through his jacket you could see he had an extremely chiseled frame. Marjorie noticed how Honey looked at him and decided to intervene.

"Honey, now you know he's trouble. That kind of man ain't gon' be no fool like Edmund."

Honey replied deceptively, "I believe you, but that was before he met me."

The girls leaned in to each other with a giggle and walked away as Marjorie warned Honey with her eyes.

The next few months passed at a whirlwind pace between work, the parties and Saturday nights. Honey hadn't seen much of Edmund after she'd hinted to him that she wanted a Mink stall like one of the big time numbers men had given his woman, so he had taken to working seven days a week so that she could have it for her birthday in October. Lyle had started out hard as a rock but soon softened into a puppy dog. He didn't trust Honey but he wanted to. Honey was careful in how she handled him. Lyle was a tortured spirit with some dark secrets. Honey assumed that she would enjoy the same relaxed situation she had with Zeke but Lyle's insecurities left him vulnerable in ways that could be volatile. He was good to Honey and she was making money hand over fist. He was the first man she'd known who didn't prefer to call her Honey.

"Lucille." Lyle paused as he spoke in a measured tone. "I like spending time with you."

"And I like spending time with you too, baby." Honey replied coyly as she lay across his massive chest.

"I'm not into sharing my women." Lyle went on in a stern yet uncertain tone. He wanted to make some demands but he didn't want to risk loosing Honey.

"We'll I'm not into sharing my man either." Honey stood her ground. She was not going to make any promises or any concessions because with a man like Lyle you lived or died by your word. Their relationship seemed to become more and more competitive. As cold as they were to one another emotionally the lovemaking was full of fire. The romance was bittersweet for Lyle as satisfying as it was dissatisfying and he was becoming frustrated. Honey thought of it as a game and an exercise in emotional discipline. Lyle was good to her and that was all that she needed from him. He was a gambler and a small time numbers runner. The money he brought in was good. It seemed with him that if one business was down the other was up. When he was on a roll his whole demeanor would change but now he was in a dry spell and he'd become rather nasty at times, but it didn't bother Honey much because she could hold her own with the best of them. She knew that she would have to cut him loose soon though. Lyle's behavior was becoming more aggressive and unpredictable each day. She was waiting for his luck to come back around then she would break it off. Besides her birthday was fast approaching and once Edmund had bought that mink he would want to be seen all over town with her wearing it. In her mind Honey had set the end date as the week before her birthday even if things had not turned around for Lyle.

Three Fridays had passed and the deadline had arrived. It was the weekend before Honey's birthday. Lyle had dressed to seek out another day of angles to exploit. The night before had been reinvigorating for him. He'd played in a big crap game and money was in every pocket. He'd arrived at Honey's after the After-party. Unbeknownst to him every kiss said goodbye. That morning Honey broke the news to him. She told him that she couldn't take not having a commitment any longer but knew that he wasn't the marrying kind. Lyle was shocked though he knew she was telling the truth. He wanted to make his mouth ask for more but his pride wouldn't let him. He walked out of the door with out so much as saying goodbye and Honey worried that she would see him again.

Friday had come and Honey planned to have a party of her own. She knew that Saturday would be spent with Edmund and her new Mink stow. She had a feeling that Lyle might show and he was welcome if he behaved himself. Honey felt that he would since their relationship was not built on false promises. She had never belonged to him nor did he to her. After a long days work Honey soaked in her tub. The chicken and fish detail had been taken over by Bobby and Marjorie. As a birthday gift to Honey they would get everything set for the party and play as hosts to her and the rest of the guests.

Honey awoke from a deep sleep at nearly 11:00 o'clock that night. It was time for her to dress and take in a bit of bubbly. Before she began to get ready for the party she checked to see how the chicken and fish was going. To her surprise all the food was cooked. As soon as Margorie and Bobby saw her they ushered Honey back into the apartment.

"Honey, Bobby and I have everything under control. Now go back in there and get glamorous." Marjorie ordered. "Most of the regulars plan on showing up early. So hurry up girl you might meet a new Sugar Daddy tonight."

Marjorie hurriedly closed the door after Honey. Honey smiled as she scurried into her bedroom. She knew that they were keeping something from her but she didn't mind. Honey loved surprises.

As she sat in front of her vanity Honey felt like she was on her way. She looked around her room and saw the red dress she'd bought laying across the bed she'd purchased, in her bedroom that was a part of the apartment she had acquired all on her own.

She thought to herself, "Not too bad for a little Negro girl from the Delta."

Honey checked her makeup one last time before she made her

grand entrance. She looked like a star. Marjorie had given her some soft fluid waves and curled her hair under. Honey was wearing golden eye shadow and scarlet red lipstick. Her dress was red and fit her body like a glove. She looked like a black Sophia Loren, voluptuous, sophisticated, cunningly charming yet interesting and beguiling. She still held her southern demure though it had been glossed over, in a swirl of smoke that seeped through full lips and seemed to create a screen for her to walk through in making her much anticipated arrival. Every head turned towards the door as Honey's red sequin silhouette emerged. Her body moved fluidly providing a journey of adventure and glory for the male eye. She had strong shoulders that carried her full breasts and sculptured legs that lead to womanly hips connected to a perfectly round mound of desires that tortured men and diminished the worth other women.

When she entered the room everyone began clapping and singing Happy Birthday. It seemed like Honey could hear the pounding of real live piano keys. Without any hesitation she by-passed her guests and headed right for the sound. She turned to look at Marjorie and Bobby. Then like a professional songstress she told the piano player to play Bessie Smith's *"Down Hearted Blues"*. Honey sang it just as throaty and strong as Mrs. Smith herself, while everyone looked on in amazement. They all went crazy and Honey just laughed her now signature infectious rumblings of joy.

She winked an eye at her cousin as if to say, "I bet you didn't know I could do that."

In actuality Honey didn't know if she could do it either, but she remembered staying in trouble for imitating the devils music when she was suppose to be working on the classics and church hymns. To her grandmother's frustration it seemed that no matter what she did to try and turn Honey into a *cultured young lady* Honey found a way to twist it around. At the end of her impromptu performance, Marjorie gave Honey a big hug and a satin moneybag. As the night went on into the early morning the bag began to fill with each twirl Honey took around the make shift ballroom. At close to three o'clock Edmund made his grandiose appearance. He was wearing a purple suit with a red satin shirt and polka dot tie. He looked a mess.

Marjorie nudged Honey to look in his direction. Honey smiled as if her one and only desire had been to see him. Her eyes lit up like the neon signs on 47th street, because Edmund carried in his arms a gold box wrapped in red ribbon that represented a dream. Since Honey was a little girl she'd dreamed of living in a big city, smoking Pall Mall cigarettes and wearing a real mink wrap. Honey stood still and allowed Edmund to approach her as she signaled with her hand for the music to stop. Edmund always liked to make a grand entrance and this time Honey wanted him to.

As the music lowered Edmund began to speak.

"Listen up everybody I brought a gift for the birthday girl. I was gonna wait until tomorrow but I thought it best that everyone here tonight, know that she is my girl."

He continued by pulling at the ribbon around the box as he stared at Honey smiling with selfish pride. He didn't even let her open the box. Once the ribbon was loose he pulled out a Coca-Cola colored full-length mink coat. Honey's knees went a little shaky. As Edmund walked up to her and placed the coat around her shoulders Lyle walked in, he was stumbling drunk. The next hour continued with Edmund buying drinks and loud talking. He smothered Honey and wouldn't let her remove the mink coat from her shoulders as he continued to inform everyone every five minutes that she was his girl. Lyle stood in the corner glaring with venom on the tip of his tongue. Honey eyed Marjorie to see if she could take care of the situation and when that didn't work Bobby approached Lyle and asked him to leave, and that's when all hell broke loose.

Bobby was no match for Lyle's natural brute strength and he ended up shoved across the room into the piano. That's when Lyle began to verbally berate Honey, even talking beneath her clothes.

"I see why we can't see each other no mo' Honey. I don't have no fur coat for you. Hell I don't even have a dime to my name. But I make you holler; don't I? Awe man you all should hear her and it ain't no pretty sight either. Her face gets all twisted... "

Wham! Honey slapped Lyle across the face with the full force of what the lord had given her. He smiled as the rest of the men helped Bobby push him out of the building. He put up a half-hearted fight as he stared back at Honey broken hearted. It was hard for her to tell if this entire ruckus was about her or whatever had transpired at the gambling house before he had arrived. The pity in Honey's eyes let Edmund know more than he wanted.

"Who is that Honey?" Edmund barked.

Honey didn't answer.

"I said. Who is that?" Edmund continued to demand.

Honey tried to calm the situation by whispering sweet nothings into Edmund's ears but he didn't want to be soothed. He was embarrassed and though he didn't mind being a fool he didn't want the world to know about it. It was his foolish pride that forced Honey to make a split second decision that would alter the course of her life.

Smack! The slap sent Honey spinning but as her contorted body reeled around the stinging blow produced a straight razor from Honey's bosom. She couldn't even remember slicing Edmund down his backside. The cut went from his collarbone to his ass bone. When Honey snapped out of her trance blood was spewing everywhere. As one of the men at the party ran to the corner to call for an ambulance, Honey and Marjorie went into action. As they packed Honey's things mink coat included they could hear Edmund screaming in the other room. Honey was scared. She didn't want to go to jail but she had sworn the night she went running from Mississippi that she would never let a man lay his hands on her again. The girls and Bobby loaded Honey's things into the truck. He gave Marjorie the keys and they drove off. Bobby stayed behind to clean up the situation and make certain that everyone kept their mouths' shut. He was more of a lover than a fighter but everyone knew that he was an excellent shot; trained by Uncle Sam himself.

The girls rushed home and though the sun was beginning to rise it seemed that every light in the house was on. Both girls were scared wondering if the police had called ahead.

"Do you want me to keep going?" Marjorie asked nervously.

"No." Honey seemed to say defiantly. Whatever fate awaited her she would have to deal with it.

The girls walked slowly toward the porch steps and looked at one another before ascending. Sooner than they could open the door Uncle Adolf stood before them with tears in his eyes.

Honey mumbled to herself, "This can't be good."

"Get your things packed." Uncle Adolf ordered. "Your Aunt Annie died, we goin' home."

With that announcement he walked away to transverse the staircase that seemed monolithic when Honey first arrived in Chicago but in the morning's twilight, death and distance towered above all else.

XXIII
DEATH BRINGS' ME HOME

I
t had been two years since Honey had seen the Delta or breathed in the country's fresh air. Uncle Adolf had just taken the highway 61 Vicksburg Exit and it would be another two hours before they arrived in Clarksdale. Honey lay her head back on the seat and dozed off.

"I just called downtown." Honey heard from the next room.

"When they gon' let him out?" A familiar voice asked.

"The man said in October."

Honey had returned home but missed most of the ambulance ride thanks to a sedative the nurse gave her before leaving the hospital. She'd fought sleep long enough to get a glimpse of the Winnebago County Jail. As the building slipped past she said a silent prayer and asked God for one more favor.

When Honey awoke the car was coming to a rolling stop and familiar voices could be heard. The car smelled of fried fish and almost day old sweat. They all excitedly exited the car and for a brief moment forgot about the tragic event that brought them home as they hugged and smiled in greeting one another. Honey ran to Verna and scooped the child up into her arms. She was a big girl now nearly eight years old. Verna was happy to see her mother but there was a distance between them that nagged at Honey though she knew that she should not expect more. She looked up and could see her grandmother standing on the porch with her cane waiting. First Uncle Adolf shot up the stairs as he called out to his Mama like a small boy though he was almost an elderly man himself. She took him in her arms and rocked him with her four-foot frame like he was a baby. They both cried and held their embrace for what seemed like an eternity. As everyone began to gather around them they let go. Then to Honey's surprised her grandmother grabbed her in the same embrace and cried aloud. Honey could tell that she was not only mourning for Aunt Annie but happy to have her home too. Then the little woman took Honey and Adolf by the hand and led them into the house.

The boys took Honey's bags to her old room and everything was just as she had left it. She smiled as she looked around. Her little cousin Bozo asked if she were home to stay with all the bags she had brought. Honey just smiled and sent him out of the room so that she could freshen up. Marjorie knocked on the bathroom door.

"Honey will you be out soon?" She asked.

"Here I come." Honey called back.

When Honey emerged from the bathroom she was wearing a pair of trousers and a lightweight knit sweater. She looked like a city girl and one with money at that. She couldn't fight the urge to show everyone just how much she'd changed. As she made her way down the stairs, she was met by her Uncle Bud's smile. "Hey, Honey!" He shouted. "Come give me a hug."

Honey ran into his arms like any little girl would run into the arms of their father. Everyone had freshened up and was now gathered around the dining room table. Uncle Bud said grace and they all began to pass platters and make small talk.

"Tomorrow they gon' bring Annie home." Honey's grandmother

stoically announced. The table went silent. Then Uncle Adolf spoke up. "We can bring our own home, that's why I drove the hearse down. I'll go over tomorrow morning with Bud and make sure everything is just like you want it."

Uncle Bud gave a nod in agreement and just like that her grandmother seemed to be at peace. Then Charlie showed up after super and set his mother off to crying again. He held her in his arms and Honey wondered what had happened to all the strength her grandmother had when they first arrived. Charlie continued to shower his Mama with attention for the next hour.

"Come on now Mama." He entreated. "Let's get you to bed." Charlie walked her to her room, nearly carrying her there.

Honey made eye contact with her Uncle Bud. "How's Mama doing?" She asked.

"Not too good." He answered.

"I think it would be best if you stayed down here for a while and helped take care of her. Just until her strength is back."

Honey stared blankly into space and went on to asked if her uncle thought it would be best for her to start taking over responsibility for Verna. He emphatically insisted that she not even think about it and went on to say that it would kill her grandmother. Honey felt a sense of relief even though she was a woman; she still wasn't ready to settle down. In fact she viewed her stay in Clarksdale as a brief detour in her journey on to bigger and better. She had California in her sights and planned to depart in the next year.

Aunt Annie's body was brought home the next day. The house was flooded with people from the community as they filed in and out to pay their respects. There was food everywhere but it didn't seem to have a smell. Honey didn't have a taste for anything her appetite had been lost in grief. Seeing her Aunt lying in the coffin lifeless, hit Honey harder than she expected. She hurt for the loss but it hurt her even more to see her grandmother in such pain. The anguish of a mother who looses a child was shockingly gut wrenching, it took this moment for Honey to understand the hatred her grandmother had felt for her father. Through the whaling cries and pleadings of why, the pain became almost unbearable. She had cried so uncontrollably that the new young black doctor had to come and give her something to calm down. Honey slept for what seemed like days and when she awoke Aunt Annie was already in the ground.

Marjorie, Uncle Adolf and Aunt Area stayed on a few more days then they made their way back to Chicago. Her Uncle Adolf promised to call the Rosenthal's and explain everything to them. Honey thought it would feel terrible to see them leave without her but instead she felt a sense of relief. For the almost two days she'd slept, she dreamed of nothing but the ocean. A new horizon was beckoning her to destinies call.

As the weeks went by things returned to normal. Honey had wanted so desperately to tell Uncle Charlie about her exploits, but he treated her like a leper. Honey had returned to the Delta's nightlife looking better than ever. Her first night out she met a high yellow, red hair, freckle faced, smooth talking sure of him-self man named John Fry. He was one of the few colored men who actually drove for the Greyhound Bus Company instead of loading luggage into the lower compartment. Honey's plan was to find an easy mark to finance her trip, work a job and move on to California. As it happens with most plans the road was bumpy with mishaps along the way.

XXIV
JOHN FRY

With in three months Honey was pregnant. She hid her protruding belly well with the aid of girdles but this time she did not hide it from the child's father. John Fry was a fun loving yet somewhat controlling man and Honey was not the kind of woman a man could control. She'd had a rebellious spirit from a child and it never left her. John immediately asked Honey to marry him but instead of a yes he got a maybe. He thought to himself that he'd never seen a woman like her. Most women would have jumped at the opportunity to marry the father of their child, if for nothing more than the sake of their honor. From that moment forward the relationship between Honey and John became a love hate one. He loved everything about her except Honey's uppity, pig headed attitude. She loved everything about him except his determination to break her will. Honey thought that even if she had to strap this baby to her back and walk all the way to California that's what she would do. In the beginning of their relationship she had told John of her plans but since the latest developments with her being pregnant and all, Honey knew that he assumed it was a thing of the past.

Honey got a job cooking and cleaning for a wealthy white judge and his family. They couldn't hold a candle to the Rosenthal's in style or class but he and his wife were fair people. They made their children respect Honey and she was not to address them with the titles Mr. or Mrs. nor Sir or Ma'am. To them color and privilege weren't more important than teaching their children about respect.

Every month that inched closer to the birth of their child John asked Honey if she'd made up her mind yet. Honey simply held him off by telling him that her mind was on other more important things. Her hips had spread but the corset she wore kept her stomach flat. She pulled it tighter and tighter each morning. Honey also continued to go out, though most nights she only met with John or he came a calling.

"Honey, look, I just want to do right by you." John stated softly as they sat alone in his car parked by the river. Every time Honey heard these words it took her back to Tom even though she knew that John truly cared for her.

"That's the problem, John. I don't need you to do right by me. I need you to love me. I can't be married and feel it half way. I got to want you all the way. I wanted you enough to make this poor child but you and I both know that if we married it wouldn't last long as a mouse in a cat house. We really don't even like one another. I'm too stubborn and you're too controlling."

John looked a little surprised by Honey's blunt honesty and though he knew it was true he half-heartedly interjected.

"I do love you Honey. So don't put words in my mouth. You do what you do best and speak for your self. Like I told you before, I just don't like your constant sassing." Honey pounce on his choice of words.

"See that's the problem. What do you mean sassing? Like you some bodies Daddy. I didn't have but one Daddy and he couldn't tell me what to do. I say what I want how I want, John Fry!" She said it with a deathly serious tone that quieted John who was never at a loss for words. He started his car. "I think it's time I take you home. You seem to have all the answers and done made up your mind. I'm just trying to do right by you."

Honey was getting hotter by the mile.

"Don't you do me, no damn favors John Fry cause' I ain't asked you for nan. You just remember you ain't gracing me with your presence I'm gracing you with mine."

Three months had gone by and Honey hadn't been out with John though she'd seen him. He stopped by her grandmother's house every Friday to see how she was doing and to bring some money for the baby they were expecting. Her grandmother sensed that something was up but Honey's figure hadn't changed much at all.

"Judge Lockett." Honey interrupted in the middle of his luncheon.

He immediately excused himself from the table. Honey was sweating profusely and did not look good at all. She explained to the judge that she was not feeling well and he quickly summoned his driver to take her home. The driver nervously drove Honey home as quick as he could but in route her water broke.

Honey cried out, "Oh, God please just let me make it home!"

The baby was early. The driver pulled up to the two story white home on Paul Edward street, jumped out carrying Honey as he kicked the door open shouting.

"Help, help this gal gon' have a baby!"

Charlie came running down the stairs hollering. "What in tar nation is all this noise about?" Honey's grandmother had heard the stranger's ranting clearly. She immediately started giving orders and going to work.

"Charlie you go down to the round yard and get the midwife!" Honey's grandmother commanded.

Charlie ran out the door without saying another word. She then helped the driver carry Honey up the stairs. She sent him on and gave thanks for all his help. She looked at Honey, then shouted in frustration, "Hun Lump you gone kill me!"

Honey lay writhing in pain unable to speak. Her Grandmother began taking off Honey's clothes. Once she removed the corset she could not believe the round full belly that lay behind it.

"Girl you a fool! You better hope you ain't smothered this baby to death."

Honey could only respond with heavy breathing and a plea for mercy and kindness. "Mama, please help me! It hurts so, bad."

Her grandmother ran down the stairs to put a tub of water on the stove. Before the midwife could arrive the baby's head was beginning to crown.

Once Charlie had come back with the midwife, his mother ordered him to bring up the tub of hot water. Honey's grandmother continued to take charge of the birth. The midwife could do nothing more than bare witness to another black life that would push through a womb to create generations of joy, pain, love anger and the daunting desire to do more than just exist. It was a girl and they named her Ollie Mae Ware. Honey's grandmother looked to her for some sense of emotion but only found indifference. Her arms hesitated to push the child into Honey's, but a calming spirit told her to hold on as she felt the tiny infant's life force strengthening hers.

Honey's grandmother stood and with the contempt of the hungry for other's greed said to Honey, "This here is my baby." Then she walked out of the room. A few days passed and Honey's grandmother lovingly wrapped a belly-band around her midsection to ensure that her 23 inch waistline returned. The whole family was surprised by the birth even Doll who had by now given birth to her out of wed love child by the fascinating English Professor at Tougalou College.

"Stop, Stop! Stop it Pewee! Stop it!"

Honey wondered where the strength came from to rise up out of her bed in an effort to tear the girls apart. They stopped immediately as one shouted.

"What you do with Mama's check? Drink it up."

The other retorted, "Naw, I don't have to steal from Mama, I got a man!"

"And you probably took the money trying to take care of yours."

Honey felt a deep sense of relief as the landlord who had become like a son to her intervened. As the girls were escorted from Honey's apartment ripping pain from an incision that had only healed on the surface cut deep into her soul and expressed its self in the flesh. The physical pain was compounded, by the emotional rupture in her heart; as it broken into a million pieces for the day's to come. She self medicated with morphine at the push of a button. With the state of high alert her every sense had been on, because of the latest altercation, she gave way to sedation as she wondered aloud.

"Lord, what will happen to my family?"

"This baby is over a year old now. She should at least be trying to walk." It was Honey's Uncle Bud talking to her grandmother. As Honey approached the front door through the screen she heard her grandmother reply, "Yea, I know. Honey done, messed this baby up wearing that corset while she was carrying her."

She walked in with an unmistakable attitude. The night before John Fry had tried to run her out of the "Hole in the Wall" in a jealous craze as she danced with Fred Wellington. Over the past year he'd been, good to Peewee and Honey. Neither she nor her family had to by a bottle of milk or pay for diaper.

"Honey", her grandmother said in a tone that brought here to a halt as she attempted to breeze by both she and her uncle with a fleeting hello.

"You know, your uncle Bud and I are worried about this baby. She past a year and should be walking by now but she won't hardly crawl. I think that corset you wore done messed with this babies back bone."

Honey's Uncle Bud stood by with a face full of concern. He could sense Honey's defenses mounting and decided to intervene.

"Look here Honey, ain't nobody saying that you intentionally meant to do this child no harm, but I think there may be some truth to what mama's saying. Now we have a cousin named Bo who's a doctor over in Jackson. I wrote him and he said that he'd come to Clarksdale and see about the baby. He said that when he was in the Army over in Germany he saw a lot of children with this condition."

"What condition?" Honey insisted.

"Look at here gal." Her uncle said sternly, "Like I told you, ain't nobody saying you done nothing wrong, but he gon' come and see about this baby whether you like it or not."

And that was that. Honey knew not to test him once he took on that tone of speech. He had never laid a hand on her but when he took on this disposition she always felt like he could. Honey said no more but walked away with a lump in her throat as tears of guilt stung the corners of her eyes. She was disgusted with her self, frustrated by her circumstance and guilt ridden over her selfish disregard for the life that had grown inside her womb. For the first time in a long time she questioned her choices and the life path she pursued.

A month had passed and cousin Bo had come and gone giving Pee wee the gift of flight that all children feel as they run through fields of Magnolias in the summer, or dart between the fallen leafs that swirl through fall's winds before winters' first snowfall leaves behind fresh mounds of powder to catch a playful tumble, while the rains of spring beckon the sheer force of boundless, kinetic energy that flows as freely as the inundated Mississippi river over banks that succumb to mother natures demands for rebirth and renewal.

It seemed that in a flash five years had passed. Honey felt that she was becoming an old woman as her dream of California slipped away she was thirty-four years old.

XXV
MAMA

oney was drowsily awakened by the laughter of children running and playing in the alley behind her apartment. She thought of the mischievous laughter she loved so well, and said a silent prayer of hope as she stare at the tiny dust particles that swirled around in the suns rays as it entered through the slits in her bedroom blinds. Honey returned to slumber's peaceful retreat as she attempted to count the small blades of light that had befallen her bed spread like abstract art across her feet, and she began to reminisce.

Honey watched from the porch while Pee Wee ran down the street to Mr. Catfish's candy store. She was skinny as a rail and wouldn't eat any real food. John had spoiled his only child and had two accounts set up for her to eat whatever she wanted regardless as to what Honey and her grandmother had to say.

Verna was off in New York visiting Tom and Honey couldn't help but feel a little jealous as she watched her first born pull out from the train station. On the day she left Honey had wished it were her leaving Clarksdale on an adventure to parts unknown. She and John had danced their last dance and neither of them had the stamina to go another round of verbal or physical tango. The world was calling and her spirit was restless but Honey knew that she needed to anchor herself. The anchor came in the form of Fred Wellington.

It had been a two-week whirl wind romance for him but a calculated, logically reasoned decision for Honey and in a fortnight the two were married. They moved into a small two bedroom home near the rail road tracks. He was a simple man with simple plans, but steady as a rock. The first Friday of marital bliss greeted Honey with two arms full of groceries and a little pocket change for incidentals and as a show of appreciation for all of the cooking and cleaning she had done the past week. Honey's husband wanted her to be a housewife and wouldn't have it any other way. He had placed no demands on her before their marriage, accept for that one. He had two grown boys from a previous marriage and promised to take her daughters on as his. Verna was fourteen and already a woman. Pee Wee didn't want to be bothered with Honey but was forced to spend every other weekend waking to the quaking sounds of cargo trains headed north. It took everything in Honey to keep from running out of the house and jumping on one of the cars as a stowaway. She had been a married woman for less than a month and didn't know how she could face another.

Then late one night as she slept the sound of death bells startled and awoke her to a cold sweat. It was just moments later that Honey's Uncle Bud came banging on the front door. It was Mama and she had suddenly fallen ill. Her heartbeat was fading and she was in a deep sleep. Honey rushed to be by her side and did not leave it until she took her last breath.

"Mama gone." Honey droned in a monotone that traveled on a sound frequency that took on the characteristics of death; with rigor mortis infusing its self as the blind exercise of the mournful, as they numb to meet their duties allowing responsibility to cool their blood until ones soul would come crashing down in a fit of despair. That's when Honey found herself lying in her interned grandmothers bed curled into the fetal position, searching for the warmth of a mothers uncompromising love and crying out in anguish, "Mama gone! Mama gone! Mama gone!" She stayed in that state for nearly a week before it was decided that she'd had a nervous breakdown.

Honey was sent to the country to recuperate on the family farm. The doctor had said that the country air and natures replenishing properties would fortify a broken spirit and heal a fragile mind. Honey stare dazed into the endless fields of cotton for over a month, and then slowly life began to breathe back into her spirit. Uncle Bud had stopped by and whispered into her ear, "Mama gone now Honey, but the world is gonna keep on turning, with us in it. So you might as well get on up on your axis and move with it. Your girls need you and you have got to be the backbone. Now Mama already gave you all the tools you need to do it. You just got to access em." Honey regained strength in her spirit, and will of her body. As her heart began to slowly mend the torment from such a violent assault of anguish and deep despair was assuaged away by time and duty. Her mind had to shut down in an effort to protect a fragile psyche; once its electrical circuits were overloaded by an incomprehensible power surge. If not it would have risked being torn asunder in the wake of smoldering flames and the smell of burnt copper never return.

Honey's Uncle Buddy Frank ran the family farm over in Lowndes, Mississippi. There were plenty of men around but only one was allowed to darken Buddy Frank's doorstep with Honey staying there. Even in her weakened conditioned Honey's uncles feared that she could be up to mischief. Their worst fears would soon be realized.

Alf Tannard was Uncle Buddy Frank's best friend, his most trusted worker and the father of twenty-one children, all boys. Alf lived on the farm with his wife and boys. They worked the land for a great deal more than what white plantation owners were paying sharecroppers. Every year he turned a profit though he, his wife and children all pitched in to make it happen. He was a short, slight of build, albino man with straight red hair. The scales on his skin from the constant exposure to sunlight made him appear a bit unsightly, though his mannerisms and strong sense of self pride seemed to help. He walked like a big man, with his shoulders back and his chest stuck out. As he carried out the rigorous duties of farm work his head was held high and his face displayed a sort of smile that relished in the joy of a good day's work. It was these minute and subtle characteristics that attracted Honey to him before she even knew that an attraction existed. She would sit on the porch taking in the sunshine and autumn's gentle breeze as she watched him move about. Alf would often time bark orders, but always in a stern yet respectful tone even with his children. He seemed to be teaching the skillful trades of farm work from sunup to sundown with the enthusiasm of a child and the instruction of a teacher. It started off as respect and admiration. Honey respected the fact that Alf carried himself as a man, day in and day out no matter what the circumstances. His demeanor was akin to that of her uncles and rarely had she held reverence for any man outside of a blood relative.

Honey watched the interactions between Alf and his wife who was a handsome enough woman; one would never have suspected her of giving birth to twenty-one children. They spoke to one another as two men working the fields together and not as lovers. Honey thought to herself, how sad life must be without passion and excitement. She had thought of befriending Alf's wife in hopes of reminding her of the joy and excitement in what men and women share. Honey would speak to her everyday and had a few times gone out of her way to acknowledge her presence, but each time her friendly greeting was met by a stiff upper lip and a quick nod of the head. Honey felt as if Alf's wife knew why she was on the farm and found that Mrs. Tannard found her weak or undeserving. The lack of respect could be felt in the air.

Alf on the other hand smiled at her everyday and often made small talk in the morning when he stopped by the house to speak with Honey's Uncle Buddy Frank about farm matters. Honey had begun to smile back and would even fetch him water when his wife was around but she didn't bat an eye. The end of harvesting season had come and it always seemed to bring about a sense of exuberant satisfaction with a sense of pride and self-adulation. Alf's chest sat past his chin as his nose rose in its usual pronounced manner above the heads of men who stood two feet beyond his five-foot stature. Honey was captivated by his confidence and felt compelled to express a show gratitude for his just being a man. He was a real man. The kind of man who did back breaking work; from can't see morning to cant see night; without a grimace nor a complaint, while raising twenty one boys and trapped in a loveless marriage to a woman who never acknowledged his manhood with the softness of feminine whispers that ride on the crest of passing glances that gesture toward secret places. Honey knew where such subtle nuances led, in shadowy corners and steamy rooms that hold the false promises of lovers, because love was not enough to hold them together, though it forced the tongue to tempt the heart.

Honey felt duty-bound to show her appreciation for his manliness, even though she'd been raised around such exemplary examples of manhood her entire life, she found it refreshing, coming from a stranger. Honey's time on the farm was growing short and her Uncle Bud had come to let her know that he was in the process of building her a home. It was on Paul Edward Street, across from the family home. As he spoke to Honey she stared out the window at Alf and for the first time he allowed himself to return her stare. It had been many years since Honey had broken the rules her Uncle Charlie had taught so well, but in his eyes she felt redemption. But, how could it be born of sin? She languished and lamented for another week, then they found themselves alone.

"So you'll be returning home soon, I hear." Alf interjected to break the awkward silence.

"Yes, Mr. Tannard." Honey answered in the tone of a young girl though she was in her mid-thirties.

"Well, Alf hesitated. You sure will be missed." Honey couldn't resist the opening.

"Will I Mr. Tannard?" She inquired. "I had no idea that my presence had made such an impact around here."

"Well, now Ma'am if you don't mind me saying, farm life is a hard life and the people who work the land, men and women alike have to be just as tough. It has simply been a welcomed distraction to have the beauty of a woman such as your self, to glance upon in the heat of the day." Honey felt enveloped by the charm of such an innocent compliment and decided to answer Alf with a playful splash of water from the well they stood in front of. They both laughed like children as she made a mad dash for the barn. Honey knew that he would give chase and that they would find themselves alone atop the loft of the barn.

Heavy panting followed by the erratic rise and fall of his chest then hers as they simultaneously seemed to slow and nearly stop as their eyes met. His lips seemed to curl and hers trembled as he took her into his arms with the strength of ten men. This little man handled her like a rag doll. There was no time for the soft caress she had imaged or the gentle exchanged she believed he hungered for. It was instead like an invasion, though she was a willing participant. He pawed and bent her until she thought she would break. Then in an instant it was over. He lay on top of her with sweat dripping from every pore of his body. In disgust she turned her body and pushed him aside. As Honey retrieved her undergarments Alf began to cry. It was a cry of great grief and loss as his body shook and he pounded his fist into his hand. Honey became frightened and decided to make a run for it. Then Alf grabbed her by the arm and pulled her to her knees.

"We must pray and as for forgiveness!" He commanded.

Honey wanted to curse him but he seemed so distraught, she thought it would be best if she obliged the old mans request.

"Lord, Heavenly Father." Alf began.

"We come to you with the heavy hearts of sinners. We beg your mercy and forgiveness in the name of your son. Lord this Jezebel was a mighty temptress and though I sought to do your will she intoxicated me with the spirit of her father, Lucifer."

Before she knew it Honey had snatched away from Alf and was standing in the middle of the barn floor cursing him, his Mama and anybody that looked like him.

"You are one sick bastard Alf. The only devil in this barn is you! Get thee from behind me Satin! Honey shouted, as she ran out of the barn."

"Mama", Honey awoke to the smell of Vodka and cigarettes. "This might be the last night I can come and set up your drip. They don't do nothing but keep up shit. I ain't never took nothing from you and they calling me a thief."

"I'm so tired of ya'll. I can't even die in peace! Honey moaned." She looked up to make certain that her new source of comfort was in place and began to self medicate.

"Punkin' you need to come out of there worrying Mama. You just mad cause your meal ticket is gone."

"We feed your kids Peewee." Honey heard the rebuttal as she began to drift off, sirens could be heard in the background amid the sound of a scuffle. Honey feared it was an ambulance and prayed to hold on. He would be home soon. She had bound her faith on a covenant with God and believed in her heart that her prayer would be answered.

This time it was just Honey and the coal black woman with the handsome face. "Push, Honey! You're not a little girl anymore. Now push like a woman!" The midwife shouted. Honey bore down with all of her might and pushed into the world another spirit to make the journey through the trials and tribulations of man until she would find her way home. Honey named her, Dora Lavern Ware.

"This here child is a white mans baby." The midwife seemed to accuse as she inquired.

Honey refused an answer. She just held on to her new baby girl and said, "She ain't exactly yellow."

The midwife interjected, "With that red hair and them grey eyes, she looks like a half breed." Honey finally spoke up.

"She ain't no half breed either. I'm gone call her Punkin, cause she's red and yellow." Honey pulled her bundle close and for the first time felt a maternal connection as she whispered in Pumpkin's ear, "Mama's baby."

XXVI
ONE STOP BEFORE SAN FRANCISCO

The days turned into months as they faded into years and Honey felt left behind. Most of her cousins both young and old had left Mississippi for the adventures and opportunities of Chicago, Los Angeles, and San Francisco. Peewee was eleven, Pumpkin nearly six and Honey's eldest daughter Verna was an 18 year old beauty. Verna's skin had never lost the clarity of porcelain. It was smooth as silk and golden brown like the rays of autumns setting sun. She was tall and voluptuous like Honey, yet more cunning and beguiling.

Like all of the young Wrights, Verna too had left Clarksdale for a promising future along with her husband Walter Sago. He was a farm boy who had been in the military and fought in the Korean War. While away he'd sent allotment checks to Verna though they hadn't yet married. He returned home to no savings and a brand new son whose month of conception tallied to around the time he'd been on leave but the boy looked like a white mans child or more accurately like the young half breed Van Burns. Neither Verna nor Walter ever spoke of it, but the absence of words in light of the circumstances said volumes. Ironically Walter insisted that the child be his junior and name sake.

It seemed that lately Walter had begun to catch on to Verna and things were turning violent. Honey worried about her night and day. She had tried to convince Verna not to move to the small northern factory town, but the money was good and jobs were plentiful. The city of Clarksdale seemed to be becoming a ghost town. The young men were leaving by the truck or train load, headed to northern industrial cities and making the transition from the farm to the factory because cotton was no longer king. Honey knew that she would have to leave too. She had made her piece with Chicago a long time ago and figured that the city didn't owe her nothing and nor did she owe it any thing, so that was out. She did have some tempting offers though, to join with family in Los Angeles or San Francisco. She chose San Francisco and decided to ask her Uncle Bud for help.

Honey took what seemed like a long and dreaded walk across the street to discuss her plans with Uncle Bud.

"Uncle Bud, she began hesitantly. I know that you built me that house over there to raise the girls up in, and I'm grateful for it but I think it's time for me to go."

Bud sat quietly with his hands in his lap and his fingers braided together as he listened intently. "Clarksdale is going down and it won't be a good place for young people after while." Honey continued. "I want to take the girls and move to San Francisco. I talked to Uncle Joe's daughters and they say that there are plenty of jobs, housing and opportunity. I also want to go and check on Verna. That farm boy of hers seems to be getting, right citified."

Bud rose slowly and walked over to the window in the living room.

"What them gal's fathers say about them leaving?" Bud inquired.

"I haven't told them yet." Honey whispered.

"You know it's only right that you do." Bud seemed to instruct rather than suggest.

"I will!" Honey quickly complied as a slight smile began to curl her lips.

"So when you plan on leaving?"

"In about two weeks." Honey answered now in a self assured tone.

"Well, I'll come by tomorrow and get the girls sizes for shoes. It gets cold where ya'll goin' and they gon' need coats. I'll go by J.C. Penney's and pick out some coats and warm clothes."

Uncle Bud was all business and once he wrapped his mind around the idea of Honey leaving again, he set out to making sure that she and the girls would be fine. He quickly turned from the window and grabbed his hat off the kitchen table as he headed for the door. Honey could see that his lips were pursed and his eyes were blinking rapidly. It hurt her to hurt him, but she had to get out of Clarksdale. It seemed that the very air she breathed in this town was slowly killing her.

There was a great sense of anxiety through out the south. It seemed that the more blacks begged for a place at the table the harder the white man beat them. They prayed for change and it seemed that god had forsaken them. Then blacks seemed to all at once decide that perhaps it was time to stop begging and praying. They would do something and that something was to move, whether it would be north or west they would move. There was promise held in the great northern foundries and factories that Delta share cropping and domestic work couldn't compete with. Most of the young folks of the day thought that any man or woman who stayed behind to suffer the continued legacy of Jim Crow was either crazy, Uncle Tom or scared. Honey knew that none of those classifications fit her. It seemed that over the last five years northern factories had been sending white men to retrieve young black men and boys by the truck load to come work. It almost appeared that no one had returned and in fact this was how Verna's husband had first traveled north. In less than a years' time Honey's son-in-law Walter had purchased a truck to carry his new wife and child to there newly purchased shack in Rockford, Illinois. The home wasn't much but it was more than they'd had in Clarksdale.

The week had passed without incident and on Friday, Uncle Bud had shown up as usual with a bag of groceries and candy for the girls. He pulled a strand of yarn from his pockets and began to measure Peewee's and Pumpkin's feet. That Saturday afternoon he returned with two knew pairs of shoes for the girls and gave them one pair of boots each. He also carried an arm load of warm clothes and two wool coats. The girls thought it was Christmas. Honey thought that there was no time like the present to let the girls know that they were moving to San Francisco, but first they would stop in a little town called Rockford, Illinois to visit their oldest sister Verna and their nephew June.

After another week of ambulance rides and doctors visits Lucille's present conditions allowed her to settle into familiar surroundings from the past that placed her at the time of her final farewell to the Delta. This time it would be the last time, she promised herself as she stood on the Illinois Central boarding platform. Honey and her girls were going in style, with new clothes and bags. She'd given birth to three beautiful daughters and was leaving Clarksdale without any regrets. She had sent word to Alf that she was leaving and hadn't received as much as a reply. He'd not purchased Punkin a diaper or can of milk in all this time.

John Fry on the other hand stood on the platform alongside Honey's Uncle Bud. He never made a difference in the girls and treated Punkin like she was his. He gave both girls a little pocket money for the trip and gave Honey enough to start a new life in San Francisco. Honey looked at him now and wondered why she never married this man. She had wanted to but felt at the time that he was too controlling and that she would end up trapped in Clarksdale. She never dreamed that her grandmother would be gone and that had changed everything. Honey knew that she would have been gone seven years earlier were it not for her death. John held both girls in his arms as the engineer made the final boarding call. Honey's Uncle Bud embraced her as if she would never return but went on to reassure her that the little two bedroom home he'd built for her would always be waiting.

Then in an act of quiet desperation John grabbed a hold of Honey and whispered in her ear, "Stay, I will take care of you and the girls. You will never have to worry if you just stay." Honey didn't answer and waited for him to loosen his hold. She beckoned the girls to bid their farewells. "Goodbye, Uncle." She waved as her eyes began to tear. She only acknowledged John with the nod of her head as she turned to board the train with two little ones in tow. She was finally closing the Clarksdale chapter of her life for good.

XXVII
LAST STOP ROCKFORD

Whoo! Whoo! Whoo! Whoo! "Last stop Rockford!" The train began to slow and the friction of metal meeting metal startled Honey to gather the girls. As soon as Honey stood and looked out the window, she could see Verna pregnant holding June. She was peering into the windows looking with excitement. "Honey Lump! Peewee! Punkin!" Verna shouted in pure exhilaration as she jumped up and down. Peewee ran out from Honey and dashed into Verna's arms, then she reached up for her beautiful nephew June. He looked just like a little Indian boy now, with sunset golden brown skin and two long silky pony tails. He smiled as soon as he saw Honey Lump.

"Hey, Punkin!" Verna called out as she hugged and kissed her little sister.

"Mother Ware how was the trip?" She asked Honey.

"It was fine." Honey answered but the way her eldest child addressed her was reminiscent of how things used to be. With Honey living a life of fancy as her grandmother raised her daughters. She remembered the day her grandmother made Verna start calling her Mother Ware.

Honey had chastised Verna who was maybe a girl of eleven or twelve years old. Verna retorted, "Honey you ain't my Mama and I don't have to do what you say!" That was the first and last time Verna had to feel the wrath of the little four foot frame that housed Millie Wright and when she finished, from that day forward Verna always addressed Honey as Mother Ware. The formality always made Honey feel a little awkward but it reminded her of how she had failed her first two daughters, though it empowered her with a sense of duty to stand with them now. She didn't want Verna to get married so young but she held her tongue. Honey didn't feel that she'd earned the right to raise any real hell about the situation like her grandmother did with her though she wanted to.

Verna picked them up in an old beat up pickup truck. The five of them rode bunched up in the cab. It didn't take long to arrive at Verna's and Walter's place. By looking at the outside Honey didn't want to see more. The house was a shack that seemed to lean over to the left side. Honey's blood was boiling but she kept her peace. The Wrights' did not live like this, she thought. The girls even hesitated as they approached the porch steps. Verna stood ahead of them on the porch beckoning them to come on. When they entered, the inside of the shake looked like an oasis in the middle of a desert. There were two golden crush velvet couches and a coffee table as soon as you entered the door and behind one of the couches hung a golden framed mirror. The floors were covered by the most beautiful, lush evergreen carpet Honey had ever seen. The house was spotless and the air smelled of pine, strawberries and apples. The lights were dim as candles and incense burned all around. The two young girls looked at Honey as they eased into the room. "Come on in Mother Ware, you all make your selves at home."

The girls sat down on the crush velvet couch and ran their hands across the material in wonder. Honey looked all around the room, wondering if this immaculate room was really housed by the shack of a home they'd entered.

Honey Lump and the girls had arrived on Thursday and it was now Sunday evening. This was the first time she had seen her son in-law. She'd asked Verna about him everyday and based on her vague responses Honey knew that there was trouble in paradise. Verna had seemed to become fairly domesticated. She kept a spotless home, and cooked three meals a day. She spent all of her time caring for June and waiting for his playmate to arrive. Honey had never seen her eldest child in such a shape and didn't care for it. Honey had long believed that marriage and children forced women to operate from a position of weakness. She had sworn to herself that she would never be that woman, and Honey kept her promise.

When Walter came in that Sunday he stunk of women and alcohol. He greeted Honey and the girls with a big grin and a basket of fruit. The girls were happy to see him. They had always loved Walter. In the past he had been good for Verna and good to her as well. There were hugs and cheers. Then suddenly the room erupted into a tornado carried along by the violent winds of Verna's angry shouts and curses. As Walter fiercely charged in thunders rage, he trampled all that stood in between him and his pregnant wife. Then as all tornados do, the storm lifted leaving the room eerily quiet, with Walter pinned to the wall as a straight razor lay against his throat. Verna lay coward down on the couch shielding her pregnant belly with June and Punkin. The furniture was strewn all around and broken glass lay everywhere.

Honey broke her silence with a blood curdling warning as she continued to press Walter against the broken mirror on the wall.

"Walter I will kill you dead as you got to die if you ever lay a hand on Verna again."

"I'm sorry Mother Ware." Walter stuttered as his tongue fumbled around for an apology. Honey gave him a stare that dared him to breathe then let up off of his throat. Walter cut and run as quickly as he could get out the front door. When Honey looked down she notice a skinny little figure standing by her side ready to take on a giant of a man with her mother, it was Peewee.

What should have been a months stay turned into an entire winter after Verna gave birth to a new baby girl. Honey made a belly band from a sheet and Verna's figure was on the mend. Walter had returned home after spending a week at his mothers. He ate some humble pie and after that things' between he and Honey returned to normal. Honey and the girls slept on palettes on the floor all winter long. As spring approached they all began to sense a feeling of not being welcome. Honey had spent nearly all of the money she was suppose to travel with to San Francisco on groceries and heavier coats for the girls.

Tensions in the house began to erupt once Honey's money completely ran out. Honey felt used and helpless. She had her two young girls and was depending on others to feed them. After a night of confrontations Honey promised Verna and Walter she would be out in one week. The very next day Honey went out looking for a job and was hired in house keeping at the hospital. Her first day on the job she met a lady that introduced her to another lady and by the end of the week she and the girls took a room at a rooming house.

Honey winced as her body was jostled about by the paramedics. There had been a rift of paramount proportions in the past week that had landed Honey in the hospital she'd worked in for nearly twenty years. Upon her release she was taken to her youngest daughter's home. It seemed that immediately the rules were laid down. She would be able to receive visits from one of her daughters. There had been a fight that resulted in the police and an ambulance being called. One daughter had a peace bond on the other one and Honey could only wonder how it all ended up this way. Her new residence was a second floor apartment that'd been made from a single family home. It reminded her of the rooming house that had taken her and the girls in so many years ago. For the first time in her life she was totally rendered helpless. In her anguish she decided to self medicate in anticipation of her knight in shining armor.

XXVIII
IT WILL DO

Honey began to live a settled life. Her days began at four-o'clock in the morning and ended at three-o'clock in the afternoon. She arrived home just after the girls returned from school and immediately began to prepare dinner. She had finally resigned herself to the daily rigors of a monotonous existence. It began as a struggle but later became a labor of love. She spoiled Punkin and counted on Peewee as her right hand. Her middle child was dependable, capable and resourceful. All three of her girls were natural beauties. Peewee had an elegant softness of perfect features, gentle eyes and a slender figure with ample bosoms. Verna had always been a flawless vision with skin that glowed like her father's and permeated Indian summer red hues like her mothers. Punkin was a petite wonder, with movie star eyes an infectious laugh and wit quick as lightning.

When Honey looked at her girls she thought about all of the things her grandmother had told her. She wanted them to choose men of means. She felt that it was too late for Verna but she could shape and mold these last two into the kind of women that would never settle for less. She thought about all of the things she'd learned from her uncle Charlie and said to herself, "My girls can have it all and not have to work for it." They just have to choose wisely and I will teach them how to make those choices.

Every couple of months there was drama at Verna's house that she and Peewee would go over and straighten out. Pumpkin went along for the ride and though she was just a baby, if her mouth could whip you, you would be well whipped by the time she finished cursing you out. There were epic battles between the mother in-laws as the two in the middle made up to break up and have babies in between the love and loss. All of the excitement chiseled away at the years and soon San Francisco became a distant memory except for the times Peewee became upset and threatened to continue the journey with out her mother and baby sister.

The family of women had a hard way to go. Though Honey had never been much for attending church things had gotten so bad she found herself in the Lord's house calling on God. She thought her prayers of a stable home for she and the girls had been answered when she was taken into a rooming house. She and her two girls stayed in one room and slept together each night. The house was dark and damp. It frightened the girls to sleep there each night and Honey knew that this had to be a temporary solution.

Within the next month a door of opportunity had opened in the form of Mama Aida and Daddy Yankee. These people were the salt of the earth. They took Honey and her girls in for nearly two years. Honey had her own room and the girls shared a room together. They had full run of the house; Honey and the girls were back to living in a lifestyle which they were accustomed to. Honey was not expected to pay any rent but she did it anyway. Even though Mama Aida and Daddy Yankee accepted Honey's money they gave it right back by buying clothes, shoes and coats for the girls; and not the cheap stuff either but the good stuff from Gold Blatts and J.C. Penny's. They treated Honey and the girls like family, looking out for them and nurturing them with love, while constantly giving words of encouragement and sound advice. The girls were thriving and Honey was able to save money.

Through Mama Aida Honey and the girls met an interesting cast of characters. Mama Aida's brother Columbus Welks and his wife Aunt Georgia owned a rooming house and Honey quickly made friends with them. She spent most of her weekends at their place playing cards and talking trash. She more often than not left the card table with somebody's pay check or at least an ample portion. Peewee made money for herself and the household babysitting. Most of the blacks that had moved to Rockford had come from the south to work in the plants and had few relatives there with them. So, they'd began to form new families that consisted of friends that became brothers, sisters and cousins depending on how tight a bond they'd formed. Honey was not one to participate in claiming folks but she had met some good people and she knew it.

Aunt Georgia was a big woman who was light on her feet and cunning as a fox with the men. She was married to a weasel of a man the kids called Uncle Columbus and he loved her dirty drawers. Uncle Columbus had a blind eye when it came to Aunt Georgia's indiscretions. The men paid her handsomely for her time and new to respect her home because as hard as she loved was as hard as she fought. Little Georgia as she was called by her peers was known to have the strength of ten men when someone disrespected one of her house parties. While Columbus worked in the foundry she lived a double life. It usually started with a dance as she twirled around the living room, seductively enticing all in her presence. Their home was party central and there were always plenty of money men around. At any given time Aunt Georgia and Uncle Columbus took in four borders, all men who worked in the factories, usually green and fresh from the country. Honey had matured and though she had plenty of opportunity to run scams on men, she rarely participated and when she did accept an offer it was under a cloak of secrecy and rules set in concrete. She didn't want anyone to know anything about her personal business. Her personal motto was, "It's not what you do but how you do it." If there was one thing Honey knew, it was how to mind her business. She was now in her forties and still had the needs of a vibrant young women but Honey was definitely making a transition.

XXIX
GOD'S GRACE

Peewee and Punkin had grown into blossoming young ladies. Punkin was a miniature Honey Lump and just as feisty. Peewee was looking to grow up faster than she needed to and Honey had resigned herself to fighting her every step of the way. The time had come for Honey Lump and the girls to get their own place. Mama Aida and Daddy Yankee had been a blessing sent straight from god, but now their son was returning from the service and would need his room. Honey found a house down the street from her acquired extended family and Daddy Yankee made certain that she and the girls had a fully furnished home. He worked as a driver for the Goodwill and as soon as his truck was dispatched to a home in the wealthier section of town he took all of the furniture and delivered it to Honey and the girls. They had barely used sofas, beds, tables and chairs. It was nothing but the best and just like new.

Honey continued to come to Verna's rescue and it seemed that Verna continued to work against Honey. It was almost a love hate relationship though there was more love than hate and more guilt than anything. The tighter grasp Honey placed on Peewee the more Verna manipulated the situation by introducing Peewee to older men and allowing her to receive company at her house, while Walter was at work.

Peewee had been dating a young man named Brooks for nearly a year, unbeknownst to Honey. Brooks had been a local basketball star, but he was now a rising star in the hustling game. He gambled and fortune's fame came to visit him more than paupers' grief. Brooks was tall and lean with a smile that held the teeth of a winning thorough bred in the Kentucky Derby. He had charm and style with a flair for the eccentric. He drove a brand new Cadillac and kept a pocket full of cash that he shared freely with all of the women in his life. He was ten years Peewee's senior and at twenty-six, though a young man he was still an older man. He had claimed her as his prized possession, named for Honey Lump's birth mother Ollie she was model thin with an Olive complexion and fine features. She was young and naïve but Verna was schooling her everyday.

Then Honey started hearing rumors about Vena keeping company with a young gambler while Walter was at work. She decided to leave work early and stop by Verna's house to give her some motherly advice on the dangerous game she was playing. As Honey drove up to the small shack she saw a beautiful bolt of blue lightning parked on the front lawn for all- of-the world to see. She wondered to herself, "How could Verna be so reckless?"

She rushed to the front door and entered without knocking. To her surprise she had stumbled upon Peewee snuggled up on the golden crush velvet couch with a man. The only thing Honey could say was, "Why ain't you at school Peewee?" As she stare at the man with his arms around her child. Peewee jumped from his grasps as Verna ran into the room screaming.

"Don't whip her Mother Ware, they in love!" As Honey Lump raised her hand Verna jumped in between them and Brooks began to speak up. "I'm sorry Ma'am if I have offended you in any way. Peewee told me that you would probably not accept this so I thought the decent thing to do was to come by her big sister's house and ask for her company. I've been nothing but decent and good to your daughter. She is a good girl and I have always respected that. You raised her well. My name is Brooks." He said, as he reached out for Honey's hand. "I want to be a friend of the family." Honey looked at him with suspicious eyes, he was a slick talking character with the manners of an alter boy. Honey calmed down and after an hour of conversation Brooks had won her over.

Peewee was allowed to keep company with him and him alone, but Honey also warned her to keep her legs closed. Honey knew that Brooks was not the best man for Peewee but her fondness of the finer things in life allowed her to overlook the obvious. He was a hustler. He could win ten or twenty thousand dollars in a Kansas City card game and lose it all in the blink of an eye. The highs where high but the lows could be even lower. Brooks had been coming around for nearly three months and every time he came bearing gifts. He'd bring cigarettes, cakes, flowers and money for Honey and bags of clothes for Peewee. Then it all went wrong. Honey noticed a change in her middle child's figure. Her breasts seemed fuller and as Honey watched her neck at the dinner table there was more than one pulse beating.

"You pregnant ain't you?" Honey blurted out.

Peewee stare down at her plate as Pumpkin's eyes darted between her mother and sister. It seemed that within the blink of an eye Honey had become a mad women. She was on top of Peewee with her fists pounding and her daughter's legs flailing. Pumpkin was crying and screaming, while Peewee begged for mercy. It seemed that as sudden as a twister disappears into the sky, leaving in its wake silence and destruction; it was over. Honey had locked herself in her bedroom to cry. It was the kind of cry that is born of deep regret, failure and disappointment. This was the job Honey's grandmother had left to her and she had allowed it to all go wrong.

When Honey took Peewee to the doctor she got more shocking news, she would be a grandmother in four months, give or take a few weeks. Brooks had not been as respectful as he claimed, but Honey knew the game. She had now decided to accept the inevitable and do what her grandmother had done for her.

XXX
PRINCE CHRISTOPHER

The chill of a Midwestern autumn brought out a warmth of oranges, browns and reds that colored natures' landscape as the middle of October bared a gift named Christopher. He was Honey's Prince. His skin was rich and brown it was tinted with red hues like Honey's. He looked like a pharaoh and Honey treated him like one. She created the most sterile environment possible and never allowed him to get dirty. She dressed him like a young man, in slacks and suits. She bathed him from head to toe every day until he was twelve years old.

When the house became too small for two women Honey wouldn't allow Peewee to leave with him, and called the police to keep him. She put up such a ruckus that the Officers told Peewee to leave him with Honey and try to take him another day. Honey knew that she wouldn't. Peewee was only trying to hurt her. Honey had decided to dedicate her life to raising Christopher. He had been born at the right time. She was ready to be a grandmother and had always wanted a son. Now Honey would pour everything she had into what she saw as the family's future.

"Mama, Mama! Wake up! Telephone! Pumpkin called."

Honey seemed to use all of her strength to pull her self into a sitting position. As she put the phone up to her ear she could hear the operator.

"This is a phone call from the Winnebago County jail from …. "Chris"….. Do you accept this phone call?"

"Yes! Honey answered."

"Happy Thanksgiving Mama," Chris greeted in a solemn tone.

"Happy birthday, baby boy," Honey forced a smile on her voice.

"Thanks Mama."

"Why didn't you call on your birthday last month?" She asked out of concern and worry.

"They had me in solitary."

"In solitary! For what?"

"For, fighting!" He paused as if something had fallen from his lip that wasn't supposed to.

"Don't worry about it Mama. I'm all right. How you doing?" Chris changed the subject in an attempt to keep Honey from worrying.

"Mama gon' be honest with you. I'm barely making it. You got to come home soon. I don't know how much longer I'm gon' be here." Honey answered in a weakened tone. Up until that moment Honey had not even admitted to her self that her days on earth were growing shorter. To hear the words part her lips were emancipating. Chris went silent on the other end of the line.

"Mama I'll be home in January. I'm gon' take real good care of you when I get there. You gon' get all better. Them doctors don't know what they talking about."

The operator interrupted, "You have one minute left."

A tear ran from Honey's eyes, as she lied. "I know you will baby that's why I need you to come on home. Maybe they'll let you out for Christmas."

"I don't know, Mama they say January."

"Well, we gon' pray for Christmas! God can do it!"

The operator interrupted again, "Your time is up."

Chris was able to sneak in a quick, "I love you Mama," just before the phone went dead.

Honey sank back into her bed as she held on to the hope of one more month. She would ask the lord for a little more time.

As crippling pain shot through Honey's emaciated body she grabbed a hold of her self medicating drip. Until the drugs took affect she prayed and asked the Lord to let her finish her life's work. She had labored and fought to keep Christopher out of trouble. Honey had paid for Karate lessons and he became a black belt. She had supported his art and he became one of the finest young artists in the city. She had manipulated Peewee into placing a second mortgage on her house to save him from boys' prison when he was twelve. In spite of the fact that Peewee, now had five other kids to keep a roof over. Honey had moved in the middle of the night because she had paid bail money instead of her rent, and went to the loan shark when her social security check wasn't enough. She had placed him in private school, when public school had tired of his antics and defended him to the end. Honey still had faith and planned to use the last breath in her body to force the love she had for him to make him whole. Honey wondered as her mind slid into the not so distant past, what could she have missed.

XXXI
PECAN PIE

I t was Christmas Eve and Honey held on to her faith. She had Pumpkin unhook her self medicating drip as she sat at the kitchen table to complete one out of the last three things she wanted to do on Earth. She would bake a Pecan Pie and peal her own pecans. As Honey prepared her ingredients, she thought of her greatest life lessons, to love selflessly, fear nothing, and have faith. She had come full circle and now understood that to love selflessly is to allow the Devine to work through you. This single action allows the soul to manifest its self in the material. She had served the purpose God had wanted her to serve and learned that giving with out the expectation of receiving something in return is why we exist and it is this energy that keeps the world alive.

"Charlie was wrong!" Honey whispered to herself as she began to mix the flour into the eggs, sugar, milk and pecans. The day had passed and night had come but her Prince had not arrived. She simply thought to her self. "It wasn't the Lords will."

The thought brought her to the second greatest lesson she had learned in this life. Fear nothing because God is in control. He has a set hour for all things. To have faith was a lesson she had only truly learned over the last year. The doctor diagnosed her with Pancreatic Cancer and she gave up immediately. Now she believed whole heartedly that the Lord would grant her a final wish and she would see her young Prince in the flesh.

Three weeks had passed and Honey knew she was nearing the end. "Pumpkin, uhh, Pumpkin, call the ambulance I want to go to the hospital now. I want to see all my kids." It had been more than four months since Honey had seen Peewee the family had split under the stress of caring for Honey. The girls would have their life lessons to learn.

Verna handled death and sickness worst than Honey so she hadn't come around much and Honey understood. Honey then told Pumpkin to call Peewee and Verna to let them know she was on her way to the hospital. Honey had always planned to pass in the comfort of her home and not the cold sterile environment of a hospital with tensions strangle hold on her family, but she was thankful to have her wish fulfilled. Verna and Peewee arrived at the same time and Honey cried as they clung to one another. Honey let her eldest daughter know that she'd always loved her and that the gulf in their relationship always pained her though she understood why.

She let Peewee know that she understood why she always felt neglected and picked on but Honey told her that it was because she was her strongest child and she had to leave behind a backbone. Honey apologized for being so hard on her but told her that she would understand why in the days to come. Then all of the grandchildren entered the room though her Prince was missing. Everyone began to file out after they said their farewells for the evening and Honey said a silent prayer. As soon as she finished Peewee reentered the room.

"Mama, they gon' let Chris out tomorrow!" She announced excitedly. Honey's strength began to muster as she forced herself to sit up.

"Peewee make sure you take him by Pumpkins to get his Christmas gift, and tell him to wear it to the hospital when he come to see me."

"Alright, Mama. Now get some rest the doctors say that I can take you home with me in a few days. I'm gon' take real good care of you."

XXXII
WHITE CASHMERE

H oney couldn't sleep a wink all night. White doves came to visit and she shooed them away. The Hospital was so cold. She told her attending nurse and she brought extra blankets. Honey took the drip for pain but stayed in the present. There were no more memories to revisit. As dawn's first rays crept from behind the night she seemed to gain strength. It was mid morning when the door opened and an angel appeared wearing white cashmere. It was her Prince. They both cried and held on to one another. Honey could see the shock in his face as his eyes fell upon the shell of a figure that was now his Grandmother. She could see the determination on his face to make it better but Honey held his hand and calmed his spirit. There was nothing he or anyone could do now. God would have the final say.

They spent the day laughing and talking, reliving days that felt dire in their moment but now fueled humorous outbursts. There was the time when Honey, her three daughters and Chris kidnapped Peewee's first husband from work. He had been getting paid on Friday's and not returning home until Monday. When he arrived he was hung over and broke. They forced him into the car, and poked him with a butcher knife until he gave up the money. Then they opened the car door and threw him out of the moving car screaming and hollering. Over the years the speed of the car had crept up the speedometer to over 60 miles and hour. Honey had pleaded for the girls to stop but they all had her youthful temper. Peewee's husband was fine except for the many scraps and bruises that covered his body. By the grace of God they all lived to laugh and tell about it. Honey hadn't laughed until she cried for a long time and it felt good to feel alive again.

Christopher never left her side and kept on the white full length cashmere coat that she had given him the entire time. He dressed like Charlie and smiled like the morning sun. The haze of winters' night began to fall upon the sky. The crowded room cleared out slowly but allowed for one last private moment between Honey and her Prince. The Doves had been circling all day and now they brought the familiar faces from a time only few new of. Each visitor's kind face seemed to be an invitation of acceptance. Honey knew that the time had come. She pulled the only son she'd known close to her and said, "This is the last coat Mama gone be able to buy you, you gone have to take care of your self from now on. Promise me you will do that."

Christopher gave a nod that seemed to search for strength.

They both fell silent but love filled the void of sound as they stare into each others eyes it was understood and there would be no need for compromise in the unconditional.

With Christopher gone it was time for Honey to meet with peace. They had a conversation that took hours but would last through all eternity. It came in the form of her Mother's but Honey's spirit simply understood it as love.

CPSIA information can be obtained at www.ICGtesting.com
Printed in the USA
BVOW08s1755070416

443168BV00003B/154/P